FEAST OF FOOLS

BRIDGET CROWLEY

Hodder
Children's
Books

A division of Hodder Headline Limited

ISBN 0 340 85082 5

Typeset by Avon Dataset Ltd, Bidford-on-Avon, Warks

Printed and bound in Great Britain by
Clays Ltd, St Ives plc

The paper and board used in this paperback by
Hodder Children's Books are natural recyclable products
made from wood grown in sustainable forests.
The manufacturing processes conform to the environmental
regulations of the country of origin.

Hodder Children's Books
A division of Hodder Headline Limited
338 Euston Road
London NW1 3BH

To Father John, better late than never . . .

The Cathedral of Saint Aelred

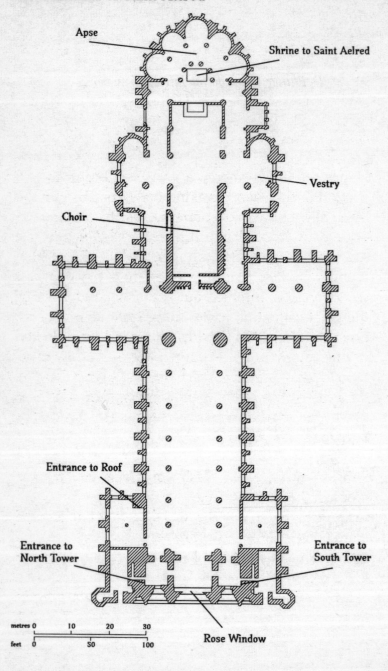

Apse

Shrine to Saint Aelred

Vestry

Choir

Entrance to Roof

Entrance to North Tower

Entrance to South Tower

Rose Window

metres 0   10   20   30

feet 0   50   100

Chapter 1

Under the frozen moon, a great bell began to toll, shattering the icy air, making the stars dance in the black sky. On and on until, across the square, the door of a wooden building squeaked open and the boys, sleepy, struggling into their long, blue woollen gowns, tripping over their feet in their wooden clogs, tumbled out and staggered towards the great cathedral. Icicles hung from its pinnacles. Frost glittered on its window panes and snow dusted its steep, grey roofs. The long, brittle shadow of its twin towers seemed to reach out and gather them in, till a door at the side opened and swallowed them up. Inside the house across the square, three boys remained.

'Wash! Go on. Now. Wash your face, you mangy, crooked little bastard . . .'

Matthew spat out the words and John felt the spittle on his cheek. He stiffened.

'I'm not a bastard and I won't.'

'I say you will, Peg-leg.'

'My name's John. And I will not be washing in that.'

1

Outside in the dark, the great cathedral bell still tolled, making the thin wooden walls tremble. Matthew's hand was like steel as it landed on the back of the new boy's neck with a crack and pressed him closer and closer to the basin. A thin layer of ice covered the dirty water within.

'Break it.'

'No!'

But the arm and the hand were too strong. The fingers squeezed and, inexorably, John's nose neared the ice. Quickly, he put out his hands to brace himself on the basin, but Matthew's other arm knocked them away and his face splintered the ice and hit the water. He spluttered, clawing the air to rid himself of the hand on his neck, but Matthew held on. Coughing, choking, red and gasping, John pulled up from the basin and swung round, flailing around with his arms, but Matthew dodged aside too swiftly and stood with his legs apart under his long, blue gown, a sneer on his broad, red face.

'That'll teach you, Peg-leg. And don't try landing one on me. I'm bigger than you, I'm stronger than you, I'm straighter than you, you gimp, and I'll tell you what to do and when to do it. I'm Head Chorister and I'll see you don't forget it. Now wash your face, weed, get dressed and be down before I kick you down.'

He swung round and swaggered down the wooden stairs. Below, the door opened and the deafening boom of the great bell surged in with the icy draught. Matthew clattered away across the cobbled square. Eyes still full of icy water, John felt around him for the damp, grey cloth that did them all for a towel. He felt it put into his hand.

'Here, Peg, dry your face,' said Hugh.

'My name's John. That's my God-given name. John. Not Peg, nor anything else. John.'

'I know. But letting him get under your skin won't make him stop. He'll just get worse. It was the same with me when I first came. He called me a weed and a runt in that voice of his, till I wanted to batter his face to nothing, but . . .' he heaved a sigh, 'he *is* bigger and stronger, and he likes to prove it.'

John sniffed and shook his head.

'And he gets in a state because his voice is going,' said Hugh. 'He's afraid it won't come back when it steadies – sometimes it doesn't. He wants to be a canon and you can't be a canon if you can't do the chant.'

'Huh,' said John. 'Some canon! A canon's a priest, Hugh, he doesn't just chant, he's supposed to be . . . well . . . good . . .'

Hugh grinned and nodded.

'Aye. Still, he's Head Chorister and that gives him a bit of power. The Magister seems to think he does the job all right. And the others are afraid of him. They've most of them had their turn at the end of his tongue or his fists. So I thought, well . . . Little Hugh wasn't the worst thing he could call me. So Little Hugh I am.'

'And you don't mind?'

Hugh shrugged.

'Well, Peg. What do you think? Will you run with it as we all do, or do you want more of the same?'

'It doesn't sound so bad when you say it. Peg. Not Peg-leg, but Peg, like that. But my name's still John though . . .'

'Aye, aye. Steady.'

Hugh held up a cautioning hand, clapped him once on the shoulder and jumped up.

'Come on then,' he said. 'Little Hugh and John Peg, one a runt and one a gimp, down to greet our Maker. Clean and tidy and not quite late, but nearly . . .' He jerked a thumb up to heaven. 'And it's not Him that'll beat us if we are.'

They hurried across the yard, their clogs ringing on the cobbles, Hugh's pattering along double-time to keep up with John's pa-dum pa-dum pa-dum. Their breath puffed smoky balloons into the crisp air, ahead of them still the sound of the single bell. The yard opened out into the wide square where buildings, houses and workshops, shanties and animal pens loomed from the frosty shadows on either side. People were already about, hard at work by candlelight or lantern or, in one fortunate case, by firelight. A cobbler hammered away at a pair of boots; a tailor blew on raw hands as he pulled on his leather needle-pad; a man passed them lugging heavy tools, giving them a brief nod as he went. Other men set up market stalls with a laugh, a curse and a clatter.

In the distance, a blacksmith's hammer clanged on the anvil and a rook cawed from a skeleton tree that dripped crystal petals of frost. John caught a whiff of the stink left behind by the night-soil man's cart as it trundled away towards the frozen fields stretching

4

away along the ridge of the hill towards the open moors. As they neared the cathedral, John slowed down and glanced up at the towers soaring up to the stars clustered round them.

'Come on, we haven't got time for star-gazing.'

John looked at Hugh and chewed his lip.

'Don't worry. You just have to stand still most of the time. Just copy what I do. Come on.'

They crept into the vestry and closed the heavy door carefully, holding their breath as it clicked. It was almost as cold as outside as they pushed off their clogs and wriggled their icy toes in their thin leather shoes. They slipped into the line of boys waiting to go out into the choir. At the head, Matthew stood aloof, holding a tall candle that cast shadows round the low stone vault of the ceiling. The boys shuffled their feet, rubbing their fingers on their legs, shoulders hunched up round their ears, trying for a little warmth. They fixed their eyes straight ahead but managed a whisper to the two latecomers.

'Whoa, that was close.'

'Where have you been?'

'Has he noticed?' That was Hugh.

'No. Well, he's said nowt.'

Then a giggle and a snigger. 'Face clean, Peg-leg?'

John whipped round, but Hugh, behind him in the line, pushed him back.

'The name's John,' said Hugh, his voice low over his shoulder without turning round, 'but Peg will do.'

'Silence!'

With a swish of his cane against his red gown, the

Magister turned on them. Black hair curling about his lean face under a round cap, dark eyes darting everywhere, he leant forward from his huge height, measuring his words.

'You will be silent. You will watch and listen and learn for Christ Jesus. What do you say?'

'We will watch and listen and learn for Christ Jesus,' they said in chorus.

'Again.'

'We will watch and listen and learn for Christ Jesus,' they said again, louder.

'Very well.'

He passed down the line, lifting a chin here, tapping a backside with his cane there. The boys stood still as carved statues. He stopped at John.

'New boy. Fortunate new boy. Fortunate to be here. Remember that. Not everyone would have . . .' He hesitated, glanced at John's foot and turned down his thin mouth. 'Well, let us just say, fortunate boy. You must watch and listen and learn for Christ Jesus, boy. And be obedient and alacritous to do well. Do you understand?'

'Aye, sir.'

'Good. It had better be so.'

He swished his cane again, then turned as a short, fat cleric waddled into the room, wheezing a little as if out of breath. The Magister took a small step back and bowed his head.

'Good morning, Canon Gwyllim,' he said.

'Good morning, Magister. Young gentlemen . . .' The Canon nodded at the boys. 'Are we all ready to give thanks to God for the new day?'

There was a mutter of 'Sir', but the boys' heads remained bowed.

'Excellent. Excellent. Obedience and . . . humility. That is as it should be. Obedience and humility . . .' once in English and once in Latin, '. . . and silence.'

The Magister gave a brief nod and, with a little smile, Canon Gwyllim rubbed silky hands together and gave Hugh the ghost of a pat on the shoulder. John noticed one or two boys glance at each other with a lift of the eyebrow as the Canon turned at the head of the line, the pink flesh of his tonsure gleaming in the candlelight.

Another canon, immensely tall and immensely broad, with a face like iron, came into the line behind him. The boys shrank back a little, though the man ignored them.

'Canon Senan, good morning.'

Even the Magister's greeting drew no reply. Hugh made an 'o' of his lips, widened his eyes and gave his head an infinitesimal shake. This man was not to be messed about with.

Canon Gwyllim hoisted a heavy, gilded cross high above his head, leading the little procession as it began its slow, measured journey into the cathedral choir. The voices of the men choristers already echoed seemingly to heaven among the delicate tracery of the towering columns, where carved angels, each in a robe of a different brilliant colour, their gold wings and faces glistening, their gold hair streaming, flew among the golden stars that dappled the deep-blue ceiling.

John gazed up. Not so long ago, he had seen those

7

angels in the making and had never tired of looking at them, holding them. Now they were up there, newly painted and gilded, clinging to the distant ceiling. Carved angels carrying trumpets, carrying fiddles and garlands and books, each watching across the vast, vaulted space as if waiting for some great event that was promised yet had never arrived.

He glanced from one to the other, searching for one angel in particular, the last angel to be made, the angel that had brought him here . . . That day when the angel had been taken from the workshop to be put into place, he never dreamt he would be looking up like this, standing with these boys, his foot mangled, his father – his father gone. And having to be grateful for – for what? Everything had seemed so safe before, ordered, secure, but now . . . and yet, if it was God's will, as the brothers in the hospital had said . . .

But before he could find his angel, the line halted in the choirstalls. John cannoned into the scrawny figure of Fitz in front of him. Hugh lurched into him from behind. The Magister, behind them, seemed not to have noticed and they turned to face the centre aisle, heads bent, trying not to grin.

The grins faded as they stood and stood and stood, sometimes secretly shifting their weight, longing to scratch under their rough shirts, stifling a yawn. Occasionally one or two of the boys would join in a part of the ritual they knew. The rest stayed silent. The canons up at the altar went about their business with a certainty not unlike that of the angels above.

Would he ever get to learn all this? John watched anxiously, but the service seemed to go on for ever and after a while his head drooped. Tiny bells tinkled, then suddenly the great bell tolled from the tower. John started awake just as Hugh nudged him with a sharp elbow.

A sharp, vicious pain shot through his injured foot and he cried aloud. Hugh looked at him, horrified, then stole a glance at the Magister. Again, he seemed not to have noticed and Hugh breathed again. But John was still leaning to one side, his eyes closed in agony, trying to move his foot to ease the pain. Hugh edged closer.

'You all right?'

An almost imperceptible nod with tight lips.

'Nearly done.'

Another nod. He'd get to the end somehow. John gritted his teeth, breathing hard. Canon Gwyllim and Canon Senan led the boys forward to make obeisance to the altar two at a time, first Matthew alone, then Simon and Edward Longnose, the one as short and jolly as the other was lean and lugubrious, Peter Holt and Fitz, then John and Hugh. John shuffled forward. Hugh put out a hand to steady him and they both nearly went down. The Magister was upon them in a moment. He grabbed John's arm, turned and almost manhandled him down the aisle and into the vestry, where he collapsed to the floor, rubbing his foot, blinking away tears. The Magister turned and shooed the other boys away.

Suddenly a hot blob of candle wax dropped on his

bare hand. John gasped and looked up. Matthew stood over him.

'Get up, you gimp, you cripple. What are you mewling about down there for? Why are you here when you can't even walk properly? You'll disgrace us all. You're not wanted here, Peg-leg.'

His voice was low but the Magister heard him.

'Matthew, my son, be patient. Remember your own first days here. You know the history of this boy and you know your scripture. We must have charity or we are as nothing. You must find it in your heart to help him.'

'But, sir, he should be in the hospital with the beggars and the other cripples, not here in God's house. It's unnatural. People are made crooked for a reason. Crooked things are – are evil.'

One or two of the boys started to murmur. John couldn't tell if they were agreeing or not. The Magister started to remonstrate but Matthew went on quickly.

'And anyway, sir, he'll be useless in the services, limping and staggering about . . .'

'He was not born crooked—'

'It was sent to him to be crooked. God willed it. There must be a reason. That's worse.'

'Don't interrupt me, Matthew. The boy can walk reasonably well. It is not always given to us to know God's will, but the fathers of the church have given their word and we do know that it is God's will that we keep promises. The boy stays here,' said the Magister. 'Now, boys. Go and find your food and break your fast. Be quick now. We must begin school.'

Matthew flushed angrily but turned to put the candle away in a recess behind a heavy curtain. He and the other boys began to leave and Hugh bent over John.

'Are you fit?'

'Aye. All that standing made my foot go to sleep, that's all. I forgot to keep it moving and it hurt like the fires of hell when it began to come back to its senses.'

Matthew whipped round at the words 'fires of hell' and his eyes widened. He opened his mouth to speak but the Magister intervened.

'Do not mention hell in this place, it is not fitting.'

His eyes flicked towards Matthew then down at John.

'Whatever the reason, you cannot continue to create such a disturbance in that way. If there is to be trouble of this kind, then I'm afraid after all you will have to return to the hospital.'

Behind him, Matthew gave a self-satisfied little nod.

'No,' said John, not sure which would be worse, to return to the hospital like a beggar or stay here, suffer through the services and be bullied by Matthew. 'No, I'll find a way to keep my foot awake. Don't worry.'

'Your pardon?' said the Magister, sharply.

John looked up at him.

'You will call me sir. Always.'

'Sir,' said John.

'Very well. Now. You know you must beg your food from one of the canons?'

'Yes . . . sir. They told me at the hospital.'

John felt the same flush of anger as when he had first heard. What would his father have thought of his begging for food? The Magister looked at his reddening face.

'Come, John. It is the same for all the boys. They each go to one of the canons. It is the rule. Do you know to which canon you must go?'

Rules, rules. He tightened his fists. 'Yes, sir, they told me that too.'

'Then away with you and be at school on time.'

The pain in his foot was subsiding, but not his temper. Still limping worse than usual, John went out into the square.

Chapter 2

John stood at the door of the old stone house at the corner of the square. The cold seeped into his bones and the frost at his feet made his woollen hose damp, dampening his anger and leaving him nervous. Perhaps the cook would turn him away and he'd have to go hungry. But when he turned the corner of the house, the door stood open and the kitchen was bustling with heat and steam and noise.

Blackened flitches of bacon dangled on hooks from the ceiling overhead next to bundles of drying herbs. The sweet, beery smell of rising yeast made John almost giddy. Two great cheeses and a bowl of cream squatted on a window sill, and, nearby, a tabby cat nosed at the remains of a cold chicken, to be shooed away by a man in a grubby red tunic. Canon Humphrey looked after himself well. John eased himself through the door and stood against the wall.

A young lad, smaller than himself, as red in the face as his hair was red and swathed in an enormous greasy apron, staggered past under the weight of a heavy pot. He glanced at John.

'What you want then?'

'I . . . I'm Canon Humphrey's chorister.'

13

'Oh ah. What's that mean when it's out for a walk?'

'I'm to break my fast here, if the cook says so. D'you think . . . ?'

The boy lugged the pot to the fire, hung it on the hook dangling from the spit and racked it up a notch or two so that it hung just clear of the flame.

'Dunno. He did feed a chorister once before. Depends what Canon do say. Do he know you?'

'No. He knows about me, I think.'

John took a step or two into the room.

'What they call you? Dot-and-carry? Limpin' Lollylegs? Twister?'

'My name's John, but they call me Peg, Peg-leg . . . you know . . .'

Peg-leg seemed harmless compared with the names Matthew might have called him. There seemed to be safety in Peg.

'Rufus,' said the boy, cheerfully. 'Dunno what my real name is, I was dumped on a doorstep somewhere, dunno where, but Cook says Rufus means red and that'll do.'

He ruffled his ginger locks with a greasy finger and grinned. John grinned back.

Just then, the cook burst open the door, slammed it behind him and waddled in, his belly leading the way.

'God's bones. As usual. Ten people to dinner and he wants everything we haven't got. Get shifting, young Rufus. You got the pot on?'

'Yes, sir.'

Rufus glanced at John and the cook's eyes followed. His eyes bulged and his belly seemed to

14

get bigger. He opened his mouth and roared.

'Who in the name of Beelzebub are you? What're you doing hanging about in my kitchen?'

'I – I'm Canon Humphrey's chorister. I've come, please, if you . . . I – I've come to break my fast.'

'What, now? God's bones, I'm busy. Canon never said . . . oh wait . . . No. May my tongue swell like a pig's bladder if I tell a lie, he did say something t'other day.' He cast a rheumy eye round the kitchen and lit on a bucket. 'Scraps. Scraps from the Canon's table, by his charity, before they'm fed to the pigs. You know that's what you get?'

'Yes.'

'Yes, *sir*.'

Another one. The world was full of 'sirs'.

'Yes, sir. Thank you, sir.'

'I should say so. Take what you want from that and get out.'

John peered into the bucket. It contained a mess of crusts, bacon rind, something slimy that might once have been oat-porridge, a few chewed bones and an apple core or two. He swallowed hard. Maybe he would forget breakfast.

'No good turning your nose up, lad, that's what you get so you'd better get hardened to it. Here.'

The cook dipped a hand into the bucket and fished out a piece of bread. He shook off the worst of the porridge and scraped it with a knife.

'There you are, good as new,' he said. 'Put this on it' – he dipped in again and added a bit of cold bacon with only one bite out of it – 'and you'm king for a day.'

John put out an unwilling hand, sniffed the offering and took a mouthful. Under the thin scum of porridge was white bread, light, soft white bread, nothing like the tough, black rye bread he was used to and like nothing he'd ever eaten before.

'Nowt wrong with that, eh?'

John nodded with growing enthusiasm. He was hungry. The bread was thick and moist with the bacon fat. He could get used to this. The cook's eyes twinkled.

'Well done, lad. You're no stuck-up young prig like some of them boys. Tell you what, I'll keep some back for you now I know you're coming. Not put it in the bucket, like. Keep it fresh. You coming every day?'

'I suppose so. I mean, yes, thank you . . . sir.'

Rufus toiled back up the steps, slopping ale down the side of the jug.

'Careful, you!'

The cook rescued the jug, poured a little into a tankard and shoved it at John.

'There you are, boy. Knock that back and you'll do till dinner, I daresay.'

John took a long swallow and wiped his mouth with the back of his hand. A sudden feeling of well-being flooded through him. He belched and the cook chuckled. In the distance a bell began to ring, not the deep boom of the cathedral bell, but the thin, insistent clang of a handbell.

'That'll be the school bell,' said the cook. 'Best be off. That Magister can be a terror when he'm roused. Go on. Off with you.'

* * *

Chewing on the bacon rind, John hurried out into the cold towards the wooden schoolhouse, across the square and past the west front of the cathedral. All round the arches, little carved figures seemed to be running alongside him. He paused and reached up to pat his favourite, a ploughman furrowing his stone furrow round the doorway.

The other boys were racing in from all directions, all of them with the skirts of their gowns clutched about their waists, their woollen legs flashing, their wooden clogs clattering, their long hair flying, all of them slipping and sliding on the patches of ice that lay here and there on the cobbles. One went over on his backside, legs waving in the air like an upturned woodlouse, and the others roared approval. But they didn't stop; they hastened on to the schoolhouse as the bell stopped ringing. Hugh caught up with John and Fitz, the boy who had fallen.

'Come on, come on, be quick. Once the bell stops, the door is shut and we're late. And if we're late, he'll beat us,' said Hugh.

He hauled Fitz up and they raced through the door just in time. The room was shadowy and dusty and smelt of wax. A great wooden chair stood at one end of the table and John eyed a birch rod hanging on the wall directly above it, close enough to make its presence felt. The boys stood round a long table, with Matthew at the top. John took good care to find a place a little way down from him, next to Hugh, with Fitz on the other side. The Magister asked a blessing on their work and they all scrambled on to one of the benches round the table, grabbing a wax tablet as they sat.

'Your letters,' he said, and they each took up a stylus and began to inscribe the shapes in the yellow wax. The Magister walked slowly down the line, poking the cane at a slumping back, smartly tapping any hand making a mistake. He arrived behind John as he made grand, sweeping curves on his tablet with fierce concentration.

'You can write?'

'A little, sir,' said John quietly, smiling to himself without looking up.

'You can read?'

'Yes, sir, my – my father taught me.'

'I see. Latin?'

'No, sir. At least, only a word or two.'

'Read from this.'

He handed John a small book, parchment with thick black letters closely written. The edges of the pages were rough and uneven and the leather cover was worn. John took it and started to read to himself.

'You want to keep it a secret, do you? Read aloud, boy. God gave you a voice. Use it. A light should not be hidden under a bushel.'

John glanced up to see if the Magister was serious and caught sight of Matthew's face glowering from the head of the table. If he read badly the Magister would dismiss him as a dunce; if he read well, Matthew would waste no time in taking out his spite. Hugh nudged him. The other boys peeped up out of the corners of their eyes. John met Matthew's gaze straight, held it for a moment, then turned away and looked at the Magister.

'Well, boy. How do you begin?'

John frowned a little and was silent.

'Do you not know?'

'At the beginning, sir?'

The cane swished down on his hand and he almost dropped the book. Matthew let out a hoot of laughter but stopped as the Magister threw him an angry glance. He turned back to John.

'Guard your tongue, boy. There is learning and there is sauciness. Make sure you know one from the other and do not use your wit unwisely.'

'Sir. I didn't mean – sir.'

'You will begin your reading always thus: "Christ's cross be my speed and Saint Nicholas".'

'Oh yes, sir. I remember. My fa—'

'Then do not forget again.'

'Sir.'

He expected another swish of the cane, but it didn't come. He started to read. The book told the story of the falling of the walls of Jericho with the marching and the trumpets of Joshua's great army. It was a good story that he knew well. Some of the boys tapped on the table with their stylus when he finished.

'That was reading with spirit. I can see we will have stuff for the acting of our plays,' said the Magister. 'Have you acted as well as read before?'

'No, sir, but I watched the plays always when my f— before . . . and I – I liked them. I'd like to try. Sir.'

19

'Hm. We will see. Now sit down and continue your letters.'

The day dawdled on, filled with making letters and words and then sentences on the wax tablet. John listened as different boys stood up to read. Often he winced at the hiss and crack of the cane on an open hand for mistakes. He was getting tired and his foot was throbbing by the time they stood together to learn by rote a part of a service. The Latin words were difficult to remember and the meaning a blank. Only Matthew could repeat them perfectly and he looked smug as the Magister praised him.

At last school was over and they stood like statues, not daring to show their eagerness to leave in case they should be kept back.

'You will be ready for Vespers when the bell rings. And tomorrow we must elect our Boy Bishop. Saint Nicholas' Day is only five days away. It will be upon us before we know.'

There was a stir of excitement.

'Saint Nicholas, it's the best day ever,' said Fitz.

'Yes,' said Simon, his eyes dancing, 'better than Christmas, better than . . .'

'And before that there's the Feast of Fools . . .'

'There is indeed,' said the Magister with a sigh, then firmly, 'but there are those of us who see those days as simply the days the world is turned upside down. Now away with you all.'

Blinded by the sparkling wintry sun after the dim schoolroom, John and Hugh hesitated, then, with a whoop, joined the other boys as they streamed out into the square among the muck and the market stalls. Some of the stall keepers took up heavy sticks as the boys leapt and spun along between them.

'Keep your distance! Don't touch nothing, you!'

' 'Tis always the same when school comes out. Don't they teach them nothin' but readin' in that place?'

'Hooligans! Vandals! Scallywags!'

But the boys raced on, hooting and yelling, John limping along as best he could, till they came to an open space where a brazier gave out a fierce glow. The boys huddled round the fire, hoping the owner might give them a few roasted chestnuts, but their minds still on Saint Nicholas' Day.

'. . . and there's the money, too, don't forget the money . . .'

'What money?' said John.

'The money they give to the Boy Bishop,' said Simon, in a voice that implied 'Don't you know anything?'

'I know about the Feast of Fools,' he said. 'I used to watch the parade with my . . . with my father . . . Jugglers and hobby-horses and all that and the Lord of Misrule in charge. Everyone falling about, chucking things and climbing on walls . . . and ale, ale coming out of their ears.'

'And everywhere else besides,' said Fitz, laughing. 'Well, then you know that happens the same day as the plays. They do 'em after the parade, up here in the square.'

'I remember,' said John.

'We're doing one this year. Ours'll be about Saint Nicholas. I daresay you'll be in that.'

For a moment John looked pleased, then his face

fell. 'Not if I have to play a cripple,' he muttered to Hugh.

'You'd be very realistic,' Hugh replied with a grin.

'Thanks a lot,' said John, thumping his arm.

'And the day after is Saint Nicholas' Day and the Boy Bishop takes the services in the cathedral . . .' Peter Holt was saying.

'. . . and preaches the sermon. The canons and everyone have to sit and listen and then bow to him . . . imagine that . . . one in the eye for them . . . wa-h-a-ay,' said Simon, whizzing round on one leg, his skirts flapping.

'. . . don't forget the money,' broke in Edward Longnose, giving him a friendly shove.

'We have our own parade and collect money from the whole city for him – and hard luck anyone who doesn't give. Last year, the Boy Bishop got more than a pound, all to himself,' said Fitz, full of wonder at the thought of such riches.

'But the best bit,' said Simon, dribbling a little at the thought, 'is the night before, right after the plays. We all go to the Earl's manor and we eat. He gives us this great feast and we eat and eat . . . He likes to fatten us all up, he says . . .'

'There's mountains of it, specially roasted meat and figgy-pudding,' said Peter Holt, with a little groan of pleasure. 'The city beggars live off the leftovers for a week.'

'The Boy Bishop sits at the top table and the canons at the bottom and they have to wait for us to be served first.' Edward Longnose looked gleeful. 'They all had heads like thunder last year.'

'So did you.'

'So I did, and will again, God willing.'

'The Earl's steward comes to the schoolhouse beforehand with his po-face and fancy clothes and asks the Boy Bishop what he wants,' said Simon, 'like this . . .' He put his nose in the air and swanned about, swishing an imaginary cloak around him. 'Well, my lord Bishop,' he said, mimicking, 'and what is your pleasure?'

'And the Boy Bishop gives him a great long list,' said Fitz, 'but it would be easier to tell him the things to leave out – there's always much, much more than he asks for . . .'

Just then the schoolhouse door banged. The boys looked round. Matthew and the Magister were outside, deep in earnest conversation.

'Huh,' said Edward Longnose. 'I'll bet he's telling the Magister he should be Boy Bishop.'

'It'd better be Matthew or there'll be trouble,' said Simon.

'The Magister don't have any say. It's up to us. We vote . . . and it's in secret, so no one knows who votes for who.'

'That's true,' said Edward. 'I say Fitz.'

'No, no, I say Hugh.'

'Me?' said Hugh. 'Never. Matthew's been here longest. Why me?'

'You sing better than him . . .'

'You don't thump us around.'

'Nor does Fitz . . . nor Simon . . .'

'It'll have to be Matthew or we'll be for it . . .'

'Piss-pot coward!'

'Not!'

The argument looked like gathering momentum until suddenly a nearby market stall was overturned by a passing cart and a heap of codling apples rolled on to the cobbles. The boys raced to help pick them up, stuffing most of them into the front of their gowns, till they were chased away by the old woman keeping the stall. They ambled off to crunch at the apples and shy the cores with deadly accuracy at the backside of any unsuspecting passer-by, narrowly missing a dark, burly man with a hawk's nose and wearing the tall Jew's hat. He carved a path through the crowd, almost head and shoulders above them all. He turned a stern face towards them and the boys scurried away, crossing themselves hastily as they went.

The sun sank low and the shadows lengthened. Hugh and John crouched in the vestry porch, munching the apples and wiping their noses on their sleeves as the cold began to bite.

'D'you reckon it'll be Matthew, then?'

'Boy Bishop? Not if the boys stick to what they say. The Magister can't change it once it's done. Anyway, whoever it is it'll be great – and the feast too. Last year I ate so much I puked up on the way home. It was amazing.'

'Amazing that you puked?'

Hugh laughed. 'Amazing I lasted so long before I puked.'

John made a business of licking the apple juice from his fingers, then said as casually as he could, 'Will they let me go? I mean . . . I've only just come.'

'Oh surely. I was new last year and the Magister let me go.'

John glanced down at his twisted foot and drew it back quickly under his gown.

'They let you be a chorister, they'll let you go to the feast. Just forget about it.'

'It's not that easy.'

Hugh gave a sympathetic nod.

'I bet if Matthew's got anything to do with it they won't let me go,' said John.

'The Magister's the schoolmaster, not Matthew. He knows Matthew remembers the chants and all that, but I reckon he knows too he's a bully and he's jealous.'

'What's he got to be jealous of?'

'Just about everything and everyone. Learning the services was hard for him and now his voice is breaking . . . You're just another threat, I suppose, and now he's heard you read . . .'

There was a rumpus at the far end of the market. Above the heads of the crowd, they saw a stick being brandished as one of the choristers was chased away. The vespers bell began to toll and they threw their cores into the bushes at the edge of the square. John lifted his head towards the cathedral, his forehead creased with worry.

'What will I do if it happens again?'

'If what happens? What d'you mean?'

'My foot. Like it did this morning. Vespers is two hours long.'

'Try and shift it about a bit without anyone seeing. That helps, doesn't it? Stand close to me and I'll see if I can shield you a bit.'

'All right. But if—'

But there was no time to finish. The other boys began to arrive, huffing and puffing, coughing and blowing their noses on to the cobbles, their faces scarlet, brilliant and shiny with the cold. The vestry door opened and they filed in, ready as they ever were for two motionless hours in the candlelit gloom of Vespers under the all-seeing eyes of Matthew, the Magister and the canons.

'Me? But . . .' said Hugh.

'No buts, boy. You are to be Boy Bishop. You won the vote fairly and you know the service as well as – as almost anyone, I daresay,' said the Magister. John thought he avoided looking at Matthew. 'We must start the preparations.'

The boys, including Matthew, crowded round Hugh, and only John noticed Matthew's clenched fists, the knuckles showing white. The proceedings started by tossing Hugh in a blanket, just to make sure being Boy Bishop didn't go to his curly blond head. He grinned over the edge as they caught him and rolled him off on to the floor. John kept his eye on Matthew. While the boys settled down to run through the ceremony, the Magister took him to one side, one hand on his shoulder, and there seemed to be sympathy in his face for the angry lad.

Outside, after school, the boys gathered round Hugh, slapping his back, tousling his hair, giving him orders for the feast. Matthew left the room with them but didn't join in. With a troubled frown, John watched him stride off towards Canon Humphrey's house. Matthew went in through the gate and, without a backward glance, slammed it behind him and hurried up the path.

Chapter 3

In a body, the boys pounded across the square, past the cathedral, and out into the town field. They dropped their gowns in heaps on the frozen, pitted ground to make goalposts. John looked at Hugh, anxious lest he be excluded, but he was chosen, not first but not last. Someone chucked the pig's bladder into the middle and off they went, full pelt.

'Hey, Peg. You can run.'

John wiped his face on his gown after the game and put it back on. ''Course I can run. Don't know why, but running's easier than walking. It gets tired though, and standing still's worst.'

'Best keep running then,' said Fitz.

'Thank *you*.'

'Be serious. You always been like that?'

John's head dropped.

'No. It was an accident,' said Hugh, quickly.

'It was no accident,' said a voice.

The boys turned. Matthew stood in the vestry doorway.

'No accident. Oh, that's the story, all right, but I say he has a devil in his foot. He said so himself.'

'I did not.'

'Got it out of your own mouth. "The fires of hell are in my foot" you said. Only yesterday. I heard it. You all heard it. And if you have the fires of hell in your foot, Peg-leg, then you must have a devil in your foot too, for devils live in hell.'

John started to protest but Hugh nudged him, hard. The other boys looked at Matthew then back at John.

'You did say that,' said Edward Longnose. 'I did hear you. The fires of hell . . .'

'But that's not what I meant,' said John, 'not a real devil. The devil doesn't . . . I just meant . . .'

'We know what you meant,' said Matthew. 'Don't we, lads?'

The boys shuffled uneasily. Matthew beat a fist into his palm.

'Maybe we should beat it out of him. Devils need a beating.'

'No,' shouted Hugh. 'You're lying, Matthew. You know it's not true. He had an accident. His foot was hurt, hurt really bad, so he limps. That's all. Now stop this.'

'Oh, so His Reverence Little Hugh comes to the aid of the halt, the sick and the lame, does he? And to devils too, maybe? Think you can lord it over me, do you? Well, I'm Head Chorister and what I say goes, long after we've all forgotten you were a poxy Bishop for a day.'

Matthew began to take off his belt.

'Somebody hold him down, and we'll get rid of the devil, shall we?'

The boys shuffled their feet, not looking up. Hugh

started forward but John brushed him aside. He lowered his head and, charging with all his strength, butted Matthew full in the stomach. Matthew reeled over, clutching his belly with both hands and retching.

The other boys cheered. Matthew pulled himself up, gasping with rage and pain. The boys backed away at the look in his eyes as he spat on the cobbles at John's feet. John held his ground.

'I may be a cripple,' he said, gritting his teeth, 'but I can look after myself, I can run, maybe not like I used to, but I can run a bit and I can use my fists, Matthew Palmer, if I have to. And there aren't any devils in my foot. You want to say different?'

Matthew cursed and swore but had nothing to say that anyone wanted to hear. They moved away. John hobbled along, his foot seizing up after all the running. Suddenly a stone hit him, square between the shoulder blades. He spun round, almost losing his balance.

'No,' said Hugh, grabbing him. 'Leave it. If he carries on, we'll go to the Magister. If you go back, it'll be a fight and you might lose. And if you do, the others may really believe there's something wrong with you, devils or – or whatever. Look at them.'

The boys were waiting to see what John would do, some of them looking down at his foot with a puzzled expression. Hugh put a hand on John's arm but he pulled away and with a muttered 'Bastard' at Matthew, he left them and stumped off between the market stalls. He went to lean on the railings at the top of the steep path that led down the escarpment to the city far below, gazing out over the mist that lay over the distant fens. Behind him, Hugh called out, but he didn't turn and soon the voices faded.

'Well, you made yourself felt, young gentile,' said a voice.

The tall Jew he had seen in the market the day before stood at his side, looking down with grey eyes, his beard curling almost on to his chest, his tall hat covering his long, curly hair.

'What's it to you, old Jew?' said John, gruffly, surprised that the man should speak to him. The Jews usually kept themselves to themselves unless they were talking business.

'Good touch! But I like to see someone standing up for himself,' said the man. 'Specially someone who has a mark upon him.'

John glanced up at him quickly and shifted his foot out of sight. 'You'd know about that,' he said, his face flushing.

'I would indeed. Welcome to the society of marked men,' said the Jew and he touched the yellow badge on his sleeve.

'I'm not one of you. And I don't have a devil in my foot, either.'

'Of course. You are a good Christian boy, and you fight your own battles. Well done.'

With an ironic bow, the man passed John and, erect and stately, started down the steps. John watched him go. He went halfway down the escarpment, as far as the first of a group of stone houses clinging to the side of the cliff. Smoke curled from the chimney and a great quern-stone stood outside. A bronze Star of David was nailed up over the entrance. Inside the wicket gate, the man turned and bowed again, went into the house and quietly closed the door. A few seconds later, a shutter closed and then another, and the house seemed to turn its back on the world.

John stood on the darkening path alone. Behind him, the market was closing down and the boys had disappeared. The bleak fens stretched away under the mist as far as he could see, to where it lapped at the base of the next ridge of snow-capped hills in the distance. He shivered and lowered his head. A tear dropped on to the railing, freezing on the icy metal almost as it touched it. Roughly, he wiped his sleeve over his eyes, swallowed and looked up to where the first star showed low on the horizon.

It was true. He was marked too.

Down in the city below a few lights glimmered in the dusk. Once, he had gone down these steps every evening with his father, rattling down in front of him, carrying his tools, sliding down the iron railings, laughing and joking. He had learned from his father to read, to write, and to carve ... best of all, to carve. His father was the best stone-carver in the city and the angels flew across the cathedral ceiling to prove it.

And then, while his father was putting the last angel into place, the scaffold had fallen. His father had hurtled down, rebounding off the tall columns and smashing on to the stones of the choir, and the angel had fallen with him, crushing John's foot, turning him for ever from John the stone-carver's son into Peg, Peg-leg the Cripple, who belonged nowhere.

Another angry tear fell, but he sniffed and spat into the bushes. Well, Peg he would have to stay and it was better than dead or really crippled like the old men in the hospital. Marked he might be, but there were no devils in his foot, just in his mind sometimes perhaps.

He turned to run towards the schoolhouse. Across the square, the cathedral seemed to lean towards him, its shadow crossing and re-crossing the cobbles with the moon behind it. He sighed and turned away.

'Once I wanted to stay in there for ever,' he thought. 'If only I had something of his . . . something to hold on to.'

For the hundredth time he wondered what had happened to his father's tools, the beautiful tools he had made and kept in his pack. There had even been one or two smaller ones he had helped John to make for himself, ready for the time when he would be a stone-carver too.

He turned back towards the cathedral. The shadows of the towers were like two arms held out to him. He looked up at the great building and slowly shook his head. Stones, no matter how beautiful, no matter how he understood them and loved to feel them come alive under his hands, were not what he needed now. He needed human company.

Hugh.

The other boys seemed friendly enough, but somehow he was afraid to trust them. A secret vote for Hugh was one thing, but when they were with him, he knew that Matthew's wicked tongue and fists could make them dance to his tune. But not Hugh . . . and John had rejected him. Even the Jew had only been trying to cheer him up. What was wrong with him? Did he really have a devil inside him somewhere? No, he refused to believe it.

For a moment he paused. The moon shone on, and the cathedral towered above him, clothed in winter, unmoved. He brushed against a single dead leaf clinging on to the bushes and it spun to the ground. He started towards the schoolhouse, hoping that the place next to Hugh was free. He would sit beside him and the devil could – could take all the rest.

Chapter 4

John and Hugh sat hunched on the base of one of the huge columns in the nave of the cathedral, their chins almost resting on their knees.

'Is he ever coming? We've been here ages,' said John, twisting his gown in his fingers.

'He said to wait, so I'd better. You don't have to.'

'No, I'll stay. It's all right. What does he want you for anyway?'

'He said we would go through the service, just to make sure I know what to do when . . . when the day comes.' Hugh gave a little grin and hugged himself.

'I guess he'll come, then,' said John.

''Course he will. He's busy, the Magister, but he'll come if he says he will.'

'I know,' said John, pushing himself up straighter and looking round. 'Anyway, you can't get bored in here. Look at them all.'

In the daytime, the nave was always alive and bustling with people. Pedlars sold amulets and relics; priests hurried here and there, some important in their robes, others thin as scarecrows, walking with hands folded, their thoughts up with the angels. Wealthy men gathered in groups talking business, three or four of them with the tall Jew who had spoken to John. Suddenly he turned and strode out. Poor men pleading for alms scattered as he left, crossing themselves and muttering. The rich men were left, red-faced and angry.

'What's up with them?' said John.

'They owe the Jew money,' said Hugh. 'Look, that's the Earl's steward.' He pointed.

'Him?' John grinned. 'He's got fists like the hams in Rufus's kitchen.'

'He lives high, the Earl's steward. Likes a bet.'

'Yes? Does the Earl owe money too?'

'Don't know,' said Hugh. 'He might, though he's supposed to be rich.'

He jerked his head towards the group of men gathered round the Earl's steward. They were stabbing the air with their fingers and muttering, occasionally turning to glare at the door after the Jew.

'The rest of them probably owe him,' said Hugh, 'and he wants paying. That's what it usually is when there's trouble.'

John nodded.

'I've never seen him come in here before, they usually meet outside. He must need his money pretty bad,' said Hugh.

Tucked into the shadows came a constant shuffle and murmur of prayers from the line of pilgrims in the side aisle. John watched them moving slowly, their heads bowed, their pilgrims' scallop shells clipped to their coats. Sometimes they would wait for hours to go into the apse behind the high altar to pay homage at the tomb of Saint Aelred, to kneel by the elegant shrine his father had helped to build to keep safe the gold casket containing the heart of the holy man. What had happened to the rest of him, nobody knew. The people of the city only knew he had been a fine Bishop, good and kindly, and that his good and kindly heart lay here in the cathedral. They knew he was their saint and no one else's, and that he was bringing prosperity to the city. Pilgrims meant trade and trade meant wealth. As soon as the shrine had been built, hundreds of pilgrims began to visit it from all over the country and beyond, and there were plenty of people waiting to take advantage of them.

'The masons used to say that the pedlars were villains,' said John. 'They said that all those footbones and backbones and stuff supposed to be from Saint Aelred weren't at all. My father said he'd have to have a back fifty feet long and hands and feet by the dozen if they were all real.'

Hugh laughed.

''S true,' said John. 'He reckoned they were cats' and dogs' bones boiled down till the flesh came off and then they sold them as relics.'

'Ugh. Catch me buying one . . . But that explains it. I think I saw one of them at it. A while back, one of the pedlars was in a shack at the edge of the woods,' Hugh said. 'There was a terrible stink and I couldn't think what it was.'

'Did you go and look?'

'Aye. He had animal skins nailed to the door. I only got a quick look, but now I think of it, some of them might have been dogs and cats. And there was this huge vat belching out steam. I nearly spewed, it stank so bad. And there was a sweaty old rat of a man sitting on a stool, shovelling about in a box of bones.'

'Did he see you?'

'Don't think so. I legged it away fast. But listen, I think that's him over there. He had the same nasty, manky hair sticking tight to his skull like that man's got. And he's selling bones.'

The man was one of many selling 'genuine relics' to the pilgrims as they left the shrine of Saint Aelred, their faces filled with pious joy, their pockets soon to be emptied by impious rogues. The man glanced over at Hugh, hesitated, then ambled across.

'Don't I know you?'

'I – I don't think so.'

The pedlar moved a little nearer and his glittering little eyes narrowed.

'I seen you somewhere.'

'Maybe you've seen me here. I'm a chorister. We're here all the time.'

The man surveyed him for a moment, frowning a little, then grunted, moved away and accosted a pilgrim unwise enough to loiter in the nave to light a candle at a side chapel.

'That was close,' said John. 'D'you think he did see you in the woods?'

'I didn't think so, but I suppose he might have. I was out of there fast.'

'He looked as if he might get pretty nasty if he thought you'd seen what he was up to.'

Hugh peered round after the pedlar and John pulled him back. Just then, Fitz and Simon panted in, red in the face, snow sprinkled on their hair.

'Come on! It's snowing!'

'We've got a board outside, we can slide down the hill.'

'Snow's not thick enough for that yet, surely?' said Hugh. 'And anyway, I've to wait for the Magister to practise the service.' He gave a wicked little smile and wagged his head. 'Got to get it all right if I'm to be a good little Bishop.'

'Oh, he'll not be here for ages. I saw him talking to Matthew and Canon Gwyllim by the schoolhouse.'

'Mmm, better not, just the same. You go, Peg.'

'Will your foot stand sliding down the hill?' said Fitz.

'What? I'll be sitting on my arse, won't I? What's it to do with my foot?'

'The devil likes sliding down hills, does he?' said Simon.

John jumped up, about to burst out angrily, but he noticed the grin just in time.

'Dunno,' he said. 'Best ask Matthew. He seems to know more about the devil than me. Maybe they're mates.'

'Yes,' said Fitz. 'A familiar. You know, a runner between him and Old Nick like witches have, and warlocks. Bet that's what he's got.'

'A frog, I bet,' said Simon. 'A nice, green, oozy little croaker. Message from the devil, Master Matthew . . . a-a-ark, a-a-ark.'

An old lady glared as she passed them. Simon

laughed and she glared even harder. He made a face at her back, pulling his mouth wide with his fingers, croaked 'a-a-ark, a-a-ark' a couple more times and then turned to John.

'Anyway, you coming, Peg?'

Simon jerked his head and he and Fitz started dodging through the crowds towards the doors, none too careful about whom they collided with.

'Go on,' said Hugh. 'The Magister won't want you around while we're practising. Honest. I've got to stay but I bet he won't let you. I'll come out when we've finished.'

John hesitated. He nodded towards the pedlar.

'What about him?' he said.

'He's busy and I'll keep out of his way. The Magister'll be here soon.'

'We-ell . . . I'll see you later then.'

John turned and started to follow Fitz and Simon down the wide nave through the forest of columns towards the west door, doing his best to dodge and weave as they had done, but his foot seemed like a lead weight holding him back. Strange how he could run a bit, but not throw his weight from side to side quickly like he used to. He looked back to see the Magister coming out of the vestry towards Hugh. At least that was all right. As he turned to leave the cathedral, a stonemason carrying his tools crossed his path.

'Magnus! Is it you?'

'John . . . good to see you. How are you? The foot?'

Magnus's accent was still strong even after years in the city.

'It'll do. I thought you'd gone home, back to Norway.'

'I go tomorrow. There were things to finish after your father . . . Well, you understand . . . But now I am done and I go to the coast to get a boat.'

John's heart lurched and he swallowed hard. 'That is everyone gone then? Everyone who worked with – with him.'

'All the stone-carvers gone, yes. The cathedral is finished. Saint Aelred's heart is safe. There is a new cathedral building in Trondheim, so there is plenty of work. Most of us are going there, the Englishmen too. I'm sorry, John. Your father was a good man . . .' He shook his head. 'Not the way to go . . . I . . . They look after you, yes?'

'Oh, you know . . . it's not the same, but yes . . . they've taken me into the choir school and . . . I guess it'll be all right . . . different . . .'

Very different and only just all right, but one thing might help.

'Magnus, do you know what happened to his tools? I would really like to . . . to . . . have them.'

Magnus nodded. 'Yes. I'm sure. They went back to the workshop, I think. The master mason is still there. Ask him.'

'Will he remember me?'

'Sure he will. He used to say you would be a good mason one day. You must come and see us, no?'

'If only . . .'

'When you're grown, maybe.'

'Maybe . . .'

'God be with you, John.'

'And with – with you.'

As he watched Magnus leave, it felt as if God would never be with him again. Damn the tears that would come so easily still. He slipped through a tiny door in the north tower, beside the west door. No one must see his tears. He closed the door quietly behind him, shutting out the eyes.

Suddenly he remembered. This was one of the places he used to come to with his father – how long ago? He brushed a sleeve over his face and sniffed.

Narrow stairs wound up into the darkness ahead of him. Beyond was the bell-chamber where the bell-ringers were ringing for Vespers. Thank Saint Aelred the boys' choir didn't have to be there tonight. He crept up to the room, his hands over his ears to shut out the noise, one arm against the spiralling stone wall to guide him. He was inside the west front, where secret rooms were hidden in the widths of the walls and a warren of passages led from one side of the vast building to the other. He had often been up this way with his father to get out on to the narrow platform in front of the rose window when the carving of the tracery there was being finished.

He passed the bell room where the ringers heaved on the mighty bells. They were too immersed in their work to notice him and he climbed onwards. He slowed as he passed a massive door studded with metal, with a small hatch with iron bars let into it. He peered in, but the room had only one narrow slit window and he could make out no shapes that meant prisoners inside. Nor could he hear anything – no one lying about muttering and cursing on a bundle of filthy straw or scratching graffiti on to the unyielding walls. On and on and up and up he went. If he could hold something his father had made, perhaps it would stop the hurt of missing him so much, bring him closer, somehow.

Passages led off to left and right, a maze of stone high up inside the west front, but he knew them well, the spiral stairs at either end, one in the north tower and one in the south, and all the links between them, the hidden rooms and the sudden drops into space. At last he reached an archway that gave on to the narrowest passage of all. He squeezed through and, keeping his back flat against the wall, eased himself out on to a platform little wider than his good foot. Suddenly, light seemed to come from everywhere. He stopped while his eyes got used to the sudden glare of the daylight streaming through the clerestory windows even higher than his stone eyrie. This must be how an eagle felt, perched on a cliff ready to fly. All the people below seemed like scurrying mice waiting for the talons to swoop. No one looked up. No one saw him. He hugged his secret to himself.

After a moment, he remembered the flood of sadness that had made him come up here and the exhilaration left him. Behind and above him was the rose window, full of pictures from the Bible stories that he knew. Carefully, he turned, reached up and touched the cold, rough stone of the tracery, the coloured lights in the window casting brilliant reflections on his arm. He ran his hands over the stone and watched the pools of colour moving like a tiny river of jewels across his wrist, his palm, his fingers, remembering his father's hands lifting the leaded glass so carefully into place, smiling as each piece fitted perfectly the curve of the stone he had made for it.

'Hey, you! You up there! What are you doing? Come down at once!'

The Magister's voice. John started, swung round and his foot failed to grip the stone. He slipped and grabbed the single rail between him and the dizzying void dropping away to the pavement below . . . just as his father had done from the scaffold in the choir. Perhaps it would be better to let go. Easier. Less trouble to fall as he had fallen. He'd be with him then, wouldn't he? Wouldn't he? But somehow, he held on, scrabbling back on to the platform with his good foot, dragging the other after it. For a moment he stood quite still, hands damp with sweat, then, still holding the rail tightly, inched back along the platform towards the archway to the north tower.

'Don't look down,' he thought. But once he had his footing, the height didn't bother him. It never had. As he reached the archway at the end of the platform and ducked to go through it, among the crowd of faces gaping up at him from below, he caught sight of Hugh, white and shaken, his eyes wide with horror. John gave him a cheery wave and started down the stairs once more in the dark.

But at the bottom, the Magister was waiting, and behind him, Canon Senan was hurrying up the nave.

Chapter 5

When the beating was over, John didn't move. The Magister had not stayed to see it. Afterwards, Canon Senan threw the cane on the floor and left quickly and Hugh crept in to the schoolroom. John gripped his arm.

'I can't . . . I can't . . .'

Hugh drew in a breath and flinched as he looked at John's back. The wounds were the worst he had ever seen. Big weals criss-crossed the red, puffy flesh and drops of blood oozed.

'He's a monster,' he said. 'I knew when I saw him looking up at you what it meant. He – he enjoys it. He is . . . Stay there. I'll fetch . . .'

John shook his head and after a moment lurched to his feet. Gently, Hugh tried to cover him with the drawers that lay on the floor beside him, but John simply let the skirt of his gown down over himself and stuffed his drawers down the front. His hose dangled loosely and he grabbed at them to keep them up. Gradually they managed to shuffle to the door, John hanging on tightly to Hugh's shoulder, moving stiffly to avoid contact with the cloth of his gown.

'It's dark outside. If we take it slowly, we can get

you back to the dormitory and you can lie on your belly till . . .'

John shook his head again. 'And let Matthew see? No. I'm not going back there.'

'The others'll . . .'

'I don't care about the others, but not Matthew. Not till I can move a bit better. Not till . . .'

'Then where? It needs . . . but we've no money for a salve.'

At the door, they hesitated. The tall Jew was passing and he paused and looked at them with a frown.

'It's almost curfew hour. You'd best be getting indoors.'

'We know,' said Hugh. 'We're trying to . . .'

Without thinking, he put a hand on John's back. John reeled and the Jew caught him. Hastily, John pulled himself away, letting out a howl of pain.

'What ails you, young Christian?'

'He was beaten,' said Hugh. 'Canon Senan . . .'

'Him,' said the Jew. 'I see. There is blood on your legs.'

Hugh glanced down. 'Peg, it's true,' he said. 'You're bleeding quite badly now; it's running down.'

'The wounds need dressing,' said the Jew. 'Let me carry you to my house. My wife will give you a salve.'

'We can't,' said Hugh. 'If they found we had gone to your house, the beating would be worse. Your houses are forbidden to Christians, you know that.'

'Rufus,' said John, gasping. 'They have salve in the kitchen for burns. He told me.'

46

'Run,' said the Jew. 'I'll wait with him while you fetch it.'

Hugh raced away across the square towards Canon Humphrey's house. The Jew supported John as he dropped to his knees, leaning him over a boulder at the side of the path. He knelt beside him. After a moment, he spoke.

'What did you do to merit this?'

'Merit? I went up to the rose window in the cathedral.'

'Up there?' The Jew pursed his lips. 'That's very high. And this is forbidden?'

'It's dangerous, I suppose, if you don't know . . .'

'And you do know?'

'My father made it, the tracery for the window, and I was with him. I'm used to being up there.'

'So you are the mason's son. The one who . . .'

'The one who was marked. Yes. Crippled. When the angel fell.'

The Jew nodded slowly. 'I heard about it. Suffering. Such suffering. And all for . . . Well, we all suffer, I suppose.'

'You? But you're powerful. You make men angry. I saw them in the cathedral. And they're afraid of you too. Look how all the beggars got out of your way.'

'Superstitious fools. And there are different kinds of fear, young Christian – and different kinds of suffering. We heathens have our moments too.' The Jew gave a wry smile and looked at the yellow badge on his arm. 'Let us just say we are marked. But we are marked by the hatred of men, not by misfortune, like you.'

John frowned. 'Why do they hate you? My father said that . . . that you were different. You don't believe what we believe but . . .'

'But?'

'That you were a man too.'

'Most assuredly I am. Your father was right.' The Jew smiled. 'And you, are you afraid? Of me?'

'No. I might have been once, but not now . . . But your house . . . that's different, that's forbidden. I can't go there, but not because I'm afraid – of you.'

'Of another beating?'

John dropped his head. The Jew smiled and put his hand out to touch him. Instinctively, John pulled away, then looked up and kept very still. Looking into his eyes, the Jew placed his hand gently on his head, gave a brief nod, and almost at once took it away. John heard him say under his breath, 'Marked . . . marked . . .'

Just then Rufus and Hugh came flying back across the cobbles, Rufus carrying a small stone jar.

'Here,' said Rufus. 'I got it. Lift your gown.'

John held back.

'Nay,' said Rufus. 'Don't be shy. We've all got an arse and we've all been beaten, I'll be bound.'

The Jew stood up, aware he was the cause of John's reticence.

'You will be looked after now,' he said. 'The curfew bell must be sounding soon. You'd best get inside quickly. Where will you go?'

'With me,' said Rufus. 'He can sleep on the kitchen floor and be gone before even the cook is up. It'll be eased a bit by then.'

'I'll say you have stayed in one of the chapels all night to do penance for your sin,' said Hugh.

'But that's a lie,' said John.

'Better than the truth,' said Hugh.

The Jew gave another smile. 'Yes, I think so,' he said. 'If you must choose to save your soul or your backside, I think I know which is best in this case. Goodnight, young Christians.'

He walked away across the square.

'Goodnight,' said John. His voice was quiet but it carried after him, 'and thank you . . . sir.'

'Sir?' said Hugh. 'But he is a Jew. You don't call him "sir".'

'No?' said John. He knew what his father would have said. 'Well, I do . . . He listened to me . . .'

He eased his back round to Rufus and lifted his skirt.

'Here, Rufus,' he said, 'do your worst.'

Rufus grimaced at the sight of the raw skin. Gently, with his grubby finger, he spread the salve over the weals. It smelt of rosemary and something else not so pleasant, but the ointment and the cold air seemed to numb the worst of the pain and John began to relax and stand more easily. Suddenly, the curfew bell began to ring.

'Run, Hugh, or you'll be knocking at the door for more salve for yourself,' said Rufus. 'I've got him. Don't worry.'

'Yes, go,' said John. 'I'll see you tomorrow.'

Hugh still looked anxious. He began to hurry away but turned back.

'If they ask, which chapel are you in?'

'I am at the shrine of Saint Aelred in the care of the angels,' said John. 'With the angels,' he said again, and he looked at Rufus with a grin. 'Some angel,' he said.

Rufus laughed and flapped his skinny arms in their greasy sleeves like greasy wings over his greasy apron.

The back of the house was in darkness, but inside the kitchen was warm and glowing from the fire. Rufus poured John some ale stirred with a red-hot poker. He drank it standing by the fire and his head began to nod.

'Here,' said Rufus, 'lie down afore you fall down.'

He cleared a place among the ashes, threw down an old blanket and held out an arm to support John down on to it.

'On to your belly,' he said.

'Too right,' said John with feeling. Rufus began to spread on more salve.

'Better?'

'A little. It smells . . . good. What's in it?'

'Hog's grease and rosemary. It's good for burns too. And Cook puts it in the pot sometimes.'

'To eat?'

'For flavour. Surely. Listen, I'll wake you early. You'll have to hang about till it's time for Matins. How will you manage then?'

'We don't go in till Lauds. I'll go and pray to Saint Aelred as if I've been there all night, then go into the vestry looking sorry for my sins.'

'Shouldn't be difficult. This'll still hurt, but not as much.'

'Mm. What about you? Isn't this your blanket?'

'I'm all right. I sleep under the stair just through there, out of the way, as a rule. But I'll stay here tonight. It's warm in here.'

He lay down on the stone floor, put his head on an old sack and, after a noisy, gaping yawn and a scratch of his carroty hair, was asleep in seconds.

John lay awake. The heat of the fire made the wounds throb and his gown made him sweat. He undid the fastenings, then reached down and took off his shoes. He had left his clogs in the schoolhouse. His shoes would be soaked getting to the cathedral in the morning. Another reason for another beating, from the Magister this time? Surely not, if he had been saying his prayers all night. But then the Magister would know he had been out and not in the cathedral. He would have to say he'd been out to the midden. Lying was complicated, so complicated . . .

Voices. John sat up and drew breath sharply, quickly turning on to his side. He listened. Through the arched doorway a faint glow of light flickered, seeming to come from somewhere above. The voices grew stronger, but John did not recognize them, though one might have been Canon Gwyllim. What was he doing here? Whoever they were, they seemed to be arguing. Would they come into the kitchen? He looked round but in the big and crowded room, there was nowhere to hide.

Quietly and carefully, he hoisted the blanket over Rufus and crawled on all fours out of the room towards the voices. He slipped into Rufus's little hole under the stairs, pressing himself into the darkness as close as he could to the wall without touching it with his back. He could hear two or three men in the solar above him and a single candle threw a grotesque shadow on the wall opposite the opening of the stairs. Canon Gwillym's bald pate loomed back and forth as he paced about and his snub nose looked huge. Even his pale eyelashes were outlined on the stone till he looked for all the world like a gigantic pig. Still John could make out nothing of what they were saying, not quarrelling, but tossing anxiety backwards and forwards between them. Who the other men were, he couldn't tell.

At last, one of them picked up the candle and footsteps started towards the stairs. John crammed himself down as small as he could, the cuts on his backside screaming as they opened up again like little mouths. Then he remembered his shoes still lying beside the fire. No one could mistake them for Rufus's grease-caked slippers. Would they go into the kitchen? He held his breath.

Canon Gwillym was a big man but his footsteps were curiously light as he padded down the stairs, the man behind him far noisier in heavy boots. A sudden shadow swept over the wall of the stairs, an impression of a mass of hair and perhaps a hook nose, but the wall was curved, distorting the image, and it was gone in a flash. The third man carrying the candle must be Canon Humphrey himself.

The hinges of the great portal creaked. No servants were about to open it. This was a secret visit, then.

'Don't worry . . . there are ways . . . we will be rid of them somehow.'

A harsh whisper from the booted man came out of the darkness, then the sound of his footsteps striding away faded into the night.

For a moment there was silence, then there was the sound of an arm being patted and a quiet 'Goodnight and God speed'. Canon Gwyllim went out, the door closed and Canon Humphrey returned alone. He hesitated in the passageway, holding the candle high, facing the kitchen as if deciding whether to enter or no. John could just see the hem of his gown and his shoes. They moved a step or two towards the kitchen when a woman's voice came from somewhere above.

'Yes, yes,' he called out quietly in a thin, reedy voice. 'I'm coming, I'm coming. No need to wake the house.'

The woman's voice sounded again, querulous and demanding.

'I know you have been patient. I'm coming.'

And with a sigh, he started to toil back up the stairs. He was a heavy man, thickset, not fat like Canon Gwyllim but not as light on his feet as he, and he seemed to take for ever, unwillingly it seemed, to get to the top.

John waited. In the solar above, the candle went out. There was a brief mumbling, then all was silent. He crawled back into the kitchen. Suddenly he felt unsafe in this place. He scrabbled back into his shoes and crept to the door.

Rufus stirred. 'What's up?'

'There are people about.'

'They won't come here. The rest of the kitchen servants are probably all drunk in their quarters and the Canon don't come here, that's for certain.'

'He was outside. I think he was going to come in here, but someone ... someone called him from upstairs.'

Rufus grinned. 'Oh aye. Herself, was it?'

'It was a woman, yes.'

'Then he'll not be down again tonight. Not even for a nightcap or a morsel to tide him over till morning.'

'But ...'

Rufus laughed quietly.

'Ask no questions,' he said and tapped his nose. 'Doesn't stint himself, the Canon, not in any respect.'

John knew the clerics were often far from perfect, that was common knowledge, but everything here seemed wrong. And those words ... who was to be got rid of? And then – then the woman ... Suddenly, he hated this kitchen, its warmth, its comfort, its self-indulgence.

'I think I'll be away,' he said. 'I can't rest here. I'm just not easy ...'

'Suit yourself,' said Rufus, drowsily. 'What about the curfew? The watch'll be round.'

'I'll take care.'

'Take the salve. Go on. Take it. Hugh can put'n on later and we've plenty here. It won't be missed.'

They did indeed have plenty there and not just of salve it seemed. John picked up the jar and put it in his pouch.

'Rufus – thanks ... thank you. I'll see you at breakfast.'

Rufus yawned and nodded. He wound himself up in his blanket in the ashes by the fire, his head on his sack, and was asleep again before John had closed the door.

He would have to be careful. The snow had stopped and the moon slid out from behind a cloud, high and bright. The watch might be anywhere and moving was difficult. He tried to slip from shadow to shadow but stumbled and kicked a stone that rolled away with a clatter. He froze, but nothing stirred. At the wicket gate he waited. Far away in the distance he could hear hooves drumming. He peered round the corner of the house but whoever was out riding at this hour in the moonlight was too far away to see.

Where could he go? Not to the dormitory, the schoolhouse would be locked. Hugh would say he was in the cathedral if he was asked and if peace were to be found anywhere it ought to be there. Ought to be.

Holding his gown away from his back as best he could, John hobbled across the square to the west door. He leant his head on his hand against the crossed legs of a king playing a harp. King David, bony and squint-eyed, plucking at the stone strings. Magnus had made him, he remembered. They had all laughed at this king, anything but royal and much too skinny to kill any giant. But Magnus liked him and so did he. King David had fought his battles and then found an easy life, hadn't he? Well, he didn't want an easy life, just a straight one. A life that didn't mean lies and, after tonight, he had to admit, fear. Who or what was to be got rid of?

His head began to ache. He pushed himself away from King David and tried the small door let into the bigger one. It was open. He slipped inside. At the far end of the nave candles were alight. He had thought of the cathedral as dark and empty at night, but the candles made the angels glitter till they seemed to dance joyfully across the ceiling far above. Below them, quiet young priests knelt in prayer, oblivious of anything but their devotions. The nave, always so busy, so full of life and colour, was dark and still. No pilgrims shuffled through the arcades. They were all asleep in cheap lodgings or in the new churches down in the city.

The moon shone through the high clerestory windows, casting long shafts of light and deep corridors of shadow along the nave. Keeping to the side aisle where the moon could not reach, John crept past the choir and into the apse, his soft shoes making no noise even with his limp. Occasionally, he caught his breath as the cloth of his gown touched the worst wounds on his back, but the pain was slowly going as the salve did its work.

He reached the shrine of Saint Aelred. He steadied himself on the finely carved stone as he knelt down and prepared for a long vigil. He might even try a prayer or two. That would save any lies when the morning came. Behind him the priests murmured as they padded to and fro, oblivious of the moon stealing from window to window as the hours passed. No one saw his head droop and then slip down against the filigree columns of the shrine. No one heard the faint 'shush' as he slid to the ground. No one covered him as he lay on the stone, cold and cramped, his foot clenched up beneath him as he slept. No matter. The morning would be here all too soon. Here for a while was peace.

John woke. Somewhere close, someone was crying. He scrambled to his feet and listened. The vestry door was open slightly. He heard a few hiccuped words and then the brutal tones of Canon Senan's voice overriding the sobs and they stopped. A man . . . crying?

There came a grunt and a rustle as if someone were heaving himself up, perhaps about to leave. John slipped away down the aisle and out into the dark. Quickly looking round in case he was followed, he slipped under some bushes, drawing the branches together after himself, trying to settle for what was left of the night.

What had been going on in there? Who had the Canon had in tears like that? And what about the men he had heard earlier . . . what did that mean? What did any of it mean? Cold and sleepless, his head pounding, he waited for the dawn.

Chapter 6

A low whistle came from the bushes.

'Peg? Is that you?'

'Here. I'm over here.'

Hugh hurried over to him. He bent down and pushed the branches aside. John was curled up on his side in a pocket of earth.

'What are you doing there? Why did you leave Rufus?'

Carefully keeping his back away from the bushes, John scrambled out.

'Well? You must be daft, Peg.'

John grinned. 'Maybe. That's what Rufus said.'

Suddenly he became serious.

'I just ... I just didn't like that place. I didn't like what was going on. And – and I like Rufus all right, but suddenly he seemed a part of it all. Canon Gwyllim was there with another man talking to Canon Humphrey. They were talking about getting rid of something ... someone ... and it all seemed kind of – sneaky. Then they left and there was a woman ... Wait a minute, it was Canon Gwyllim! It was him. It was him crying in the vestry.'

'What? What do you mean, crying . . . grown men don't cry.'

'He did. Canon Senan was there going on and on like he does, and someone was crying. I couldn't see in, but I'm sure it was Canon Gwyllim.'

Across the square, the vestry door opened and Canon Senan came out. Canon Gwyllim followed him and seemed to cower in the doorway. He put a hand on Canon Senan's arm, as if pleading with him, trying to hold him back. Canon Senan shook him off and strode across the square, his back unrelenting.

'There must be an end to it.' He flung the words back over his shoulder without pausing. 'No delay, I tell you.'

Canon Gwyllim seemed to collapse like a pricked bladder, then, with a great sob, dragged himself back inside the vestry and closed the door.

'Now what was that all about?' said Hugh, thoughtfully.

'That Senan is a monster,' said John. 'You're right, he likes giving pain. And beatings aren't always the worst kind of pain and he knows it. He hurts people inside their heads . . . in their hearts . . . where it . . . where it hurts most . . .'

Hugh glanced at him and he cleared his throat.

'But – but there is something strange going on,' he continued. 'I wonder who the other man was? I think I heard him gallop away into the valley.'

John pointed along the length of the ridge behind the cathedral where the woods crept up the side of the hill.

'That's towards the Earl's manor,' said Hugh.

'Nothing much else that way except farms, and farmers don't gallop on horses, not at night after the curfew. And poachers don't ride either.'

'Just as well he didn't see us,' said John, 'or I'd have got another beating and so might you.'

'How is it?' said Hugh. 'Your back . . . I was forgetting.'

'A bit easier. I've got the salve. Rufus gave it to me. He's all right really. Perhaps I shouldn't have just gone off like that.'

'You're a bit of a one for going off, aren't you?' said Hugh with a rueful smile. 'But don't worry, Rufus won't care. Shall I put some on?'

John gave a nod. They burrowed into the bushes and John lifted his skirts. Hugh winced.

'It's better but it still looks mighty sore. Can you sit down?'

'No, but we've to stand all through the service and by the time school starts I'll be so tired, I won't care if it hurts. I lay on my side last night, but I didn't sleep much.'

'I'm not surprised,' said Hugh, smoothing on the salve thickly. 'No more did I.'

The cathedral bell started tolling.

'They'll all be up soon,' said Hugh.

John took the drawers from the front of his gown and gingerly pulled them on. He brushed off the worst of the twigs and leaves and Hugh started to help. With a yelp, John pulled away.

'Not the back,' he said.

'Sorry,' said Hugh. 'I didn't think.'

John looked at him. 'No, I'm sorry,' he said. 'I

didn't mean to be . . . Hugh, thank you . . . Listen, I owe you . . .'

'Shut it,' said Hugh with a little grin. 'Uh-oh, here they come.'

The first sleepy choristers emerged from the dormitory house and clattered across the square as two men arrived to put up the first market stalls. John and Hugh waited in the shadows till the boys had passed, fell in behind them and followed them into the vestry. There was no sign of Canon Gwyllim, but the Magister was already there.

'How did he get in without us seeing him?' John wondered aloud enough for Hugh to hear.

'West door?'

'We'd have seen that too, wouldn't we?'

'Well, he didn't see us either. Thank you, Saint Hugh,' he said with a glance upwards.

'. . . Unless – unless he was in the vestry all the time with . . .' said John.

He nodded at Canon Gwyllim fussing in, rubbing his hands, nodding and smiling a sickly smile that might have fooled the others, but not him. The man's face was always pink and puffy, but John could tell it was swollen from crying and his snub nose was red.

The Canon gave a subdued 'Good morning' to the Magister, sniffed and said in an unusually gruff voice, 'A touch of the rheum I think. I am not well at all. By your goodness I will leave this morning to you and the g-good Canon Senan. I . . . I . . .'

'By all means,' said the Magister. 'Return to your bed, reverend sir. You look feverish. Canon Senan and I can manage, I'm quite sure.'

'I bet you can,' thought John. 'Pity it's not Canon Senan that's sick.'

With that, Canon Gwyllim waddled away into the cathedral. As he went, he drew to one side quickly, lowering his eyes, as Canon Senan strolled in straight past him without giving him so much as a glance. Canon Senan surveyed them all, tapping his cane against his gown.

'My blood's on that cane,' thought John. 'I wonder how many other boys' is mixed up with mine?'

He stared at the Canon, almost willing him to look him in the eye, but he passed by and stood at the head of the procession, pushed the cane through his belt and hoisted the crucifix high over his head.

John looked up at the gold figure on the cross, the tiny head bowed in agony seeming to gaze straight down on Canon Senan. Beneath it, the Canon gazed ahead, unmoved. John frowned to himself and shook his head. Hugh nudged him, a question on his face. John mouthed 'Doesn't matter' and concentrated on the two hours before him, keeping his foot awake and his back asleep, as the procession began to move forward into the cathedral.

When the service was over, somehow he managed to get back to the vestry without stumbling and, by chewing his lip hard, without crying out. Canon Senan watched them leave with an unblinking eye.

Outside, Hugh held John back to let the others get ahead.

'What's wrong?' said John.

'Nothing. Just let Matthew get into the schoolroom

before us. He knows you weren't in your bed last night and he knows about the beating and why. He's not going to let that go without . . .'

'How do you know?'

'I saw him speak to Canon Senan just as we went in. And Edward Longnose said he heard him.'

'Oh, let him stew,' said John. 'I'll have to face him some time.'

They went across to the schoolroom, where the Magister was waiting. The others were making a din scraping back the benches, climbing over them, getting settled. The Magister came up to John and said quietly, 'Are you . . . can you – can you sit?'

John glanced up at him. For a second their eyes met. The Magister dropped his head and pursed his lips.

'Sir. Yes, sir. I think so.'

The Magister nodded, turned away, then turned back with an angry sigh. 'That was a wrong and foolish thing to do, John. You could have . . .'

Again John met his gaze. The Magister shook his head. He seemed to have run out of words.

'Sir!' Matthew's voice, loud and clear, from the head of the table, turned all heads towards him.

'Sir. Is there to be no public chastisement for such a – a breach of discipline?' He nodded towards John.

John had been waiting for this. Matthew couldn't let a chance go by to humiliate him. As usual, he was spouting adult words to bolster himself up.

'There has been punishment – enough,' said the Magister. 'It was a foolish and dangerous act, but John has paid his debt.'

'But sir, it's not just that. Not just what he did yesterday. Peg-leg – er, John was not in his bed all night, not in the dormitory anywhere.'

'Is this true, John?'

'Sir.'

'Where were you?'

'I – I—'

'He was at the shrine of Saint Aelred, doing penance,' said Hugh, breaking in quickly. 'He told me that's what he would do rather than . . .'

'Rather than?'

'Well, rather than try and lie on his bed like – like that . . .' He jerked a thumb towards John's back. A couple of the boys sniggered, perhaps in sympathy, perhaps not.

'I see. And did you do penance?'

'Some of the time,' said John, thankful the Magister had said 'do penance' rather than 'did you stay at the shrine', 'but I – I fell asleep.'

'Why did you not return to the dormitory?'

'I wasn't sure I could get in without . . . without waking anyone.'

He couldn't help a quick glance towards Matthew. The Magister followed his eyes, then thought for a moment.

'I think, Matthew, considering everything,' he said, 'it would seem to me that penance enough has been done.'

'But . . .'

'Enough. Sit down. All of you.' He looked back at John. 'You too, John, sit down.'

'Sir.'

Not so easy. Hugh put up a hand to help him but lifting his leg over the bench was agony. He tried sitting sideways to swing both legs over but that was painful too. In the end, he knelt on the bench, one hand on Hugh's shoulder, then slithered down anyhow, letting out a gasp that had Matthew smiling in triumph. Once in position, with his gown pulled up a bit at the back, it wasn't too bad. It didn't do to move too suddenly, but otherwise, the salve was doing its work, even though the smell was by this time a little strange.

Matthew was less willing to settle down. Only the Magister's stern eye made him start to clamber over the bench, when a heavy knocking made him stop, his leg in mid-air. The Magister threw open the door and a rare smile lit up his face. With a little bow of his head, he gestured 'Come in' with one hand, holding back the heavy door with the other.

'Welcome, sir. Please enter.'

Sweeping off his hat, the Earl's steward strode in, his brilliant garments brightening the dark little room.

'Good morning to you, Magister ... young gentlemen.'

'Sir.'

The boys leapt up, scraping back the benches, dropping styluses, pushing away the wax tablets. This was more like it. They looked at Hugh and back at the steward, nudging each other, whispering.

'Feast of Fools, is it? All ready for the Lord of Misrule then?' said the steward.

Every head nodded eagerly.

'And Saint Nicholas? Which is the lucky fellow, then? Who's the Boy Bishop?'

'He is,' came the chorus, everyone looking at Hugh. Matthew remained silent, one foot still on the bench, chewing his lip.

'Come here, boy,' said the steward. He put his hat on the table, flicked back the fur edge of his long sleeves and jumped Hugh over the bench to stand at his feet.

'Aren't you a bit little to be a bishop, boy?'

'I'm only a boy bishop, sir,' said Hugh with a grin.

The steward threw back his head and roared.

'You'll do. You'll give 'em a run for their money. My lord likes a bit of spirit. Only a boy bishop indeed. Ah well . . . Now then, Your Grace, what's your will? What are we to stuff your little belly with on Saint Nicholas' eve?'

He gave Hugh a mock bow and pushed his fist against his cheek with another laugh.

A few whispers started to leak out around the table.

'Go on, Hugh . . .'

'Remember what we said . . .'

'Tell him . . .'

'Please sir, we – I'd like er . . .'

Hugh started the list and ground to a halt. A collective groan went up.

'I don't think your young friends think that's good enough. I think they want a list as long as your arm – or better still, mine.'

'But will you remember it all, sir?'

The steward stood with his legs apart, hands on

his hips and leant down towards him. 'What's that?'

Hugh laughed up at him and the steward flicked his nose with his finger.

'Cheeky young blighter.'

Hugh laughed again and reeled off the long list of delights for his feast, with loud promptings from the other boys. Matthew slumped down on the bench and took no part in the proceedings, affecting boredom. The Magister looked on with, for him, a benevolent eye.

With a friendly parting cuff on the ear for Hugh, the Earl's steward picked up his hat and swept out. The boys crowded to the door, watching and waving with whoops and whistles, as he mounted his grey horse, wheeled and trotted away. When he had gone, even the Magister had to give up the idea of lessons.

'Well, well,' he said, with a sigh. 'We would do well to spend the rest of the day going over the Boy Bishop's service. Saint Nicholas' Day is . . .'

'. . . only three days away, my lord Bishop,' said Edward Longnose, pretending to pummel Hugh in the stomach. Hugh giggled and pummelled him back.

'Two days! Two days! Oooh, can't wait . . .' said Simon, smacking his lips.

'Everything must be ready before the Feast of Fools. Once it starts, time runs away and the world . . .' said the Magister with another sigh, 'the world is turned upside down till Christmas comes and brings the Christ child to put it all to rights.'

'And it can't come soon enough for me,' thought John. He looked at Hugh and laughed with him, trying to fight off the uneasy feeling he had when he thought of all these strange events to come. The feeling had nothing to do with his back, or Matthew, or even the strange behaviour of the Canons, nothing to do with any of the troubling things that seemed to have taken over his life for the present. Why did he wish it was all over? Perhaps because his world had already been turned upside down for ever and there was no putting it back. Who knew if, once let in, the Lord of Misrule would ever go away. He shook his head.

'Well,' said the Magister, 'let us get on with it and make it go with a swing so we can get back to normal.'

'Oh, sir,' said the boys, in voices that said 'spoilsport'.

'Normal . . .' thought John. 'Well, whatever that means, it can't come soon enough.'

Chapter 7

Hugh settled the question of who was to play Saint Nicholas. The Magister told him that the Boy Bishop had the right to play the part, but the look on Matthew's face and the sudden hush that came over the schoolroom were enough.

'No, sir,' said Hugh. 'Let someone else do it. I've enough to do and it's only fair . . .'

The Magister quickly took him up on his offer.

'Wise boy,' he said. 'Who will you choose?'

'Sir, you choose,' said Hugh, then hurriedly, 'Simon could play it or Fitz . . . or well, why not Matthew? He is the oldest and he is . . . is . . .'

While he was failing to think of one good reason for Matthew to play a saint, the Magister broke in.

'An excellent choice, Hugh, Matthew it shall be,' he said, before anyone could say otherwise.

There was an audible sigh, perhaps of relief, perhaps of mutiny, but no one raised a voice to argue. Matthew's pride was saved and that, in the end, would be better for everyone. The Magister called for a blessing on their play-making and work began.

'We will tell the story of Saint Nicholas saving the sailors from drowning,' said the Magister. 'You know we act on a dray-cart in the square? We will use the table as the cart, for now, and we will have the boat down here on the floor. Matthew, you will be on land, standing up on the dray.'

Matthew vaulted up on to the table and looked down around him, arms folded, with a satisfied grin. The others turned their heads away, as if casually, but raising their eyebrows and rolling their eyes. Fitz put up a hand.

'Please sir, what about the bit when Saint Nicholas is just a new-born babe but stands up to pray . . . you know, like this . . . ?'

He put his hands together, screwed up his face and bawled like a baby. The other boys hooted with laughter.

'Aye!'

'Go on, Matthew, act like a baby.'

'That's it . . . cry baby, cry . . .'

Matthew stamped on the table but his thin slippers made no sound. 'Shut up,' he roared, his face white with rage.

'Nay,' said Edward Longnose, trying to keep a straight face, 'that's the best bit of the story, Matthew. You must do that part and – and how he – he – he – he . . .' He bent double, almost crying with laughter.

'What? What?' yelled the boys.

'You know,' said Hugh, all seriousness. 'How he fasted too, even when he was just born. You remember. How he wouldn't suck milk from his mother more than once on a Wednesday and a Friday. Yes, Matthew, you must do that bit. That's important. I'd do it if it were me.'

Hugh's face was innocence itself, but his eyes twinkled wickedly. Matthew looked as if he would leap down from the table and throttle him.

'Hugh!' The Magister whisked his cane down sharply on the table. 'Enough. Do not spoil your generosity with this nonsense. If we do the beginning of the story, I say *if* we do it, we will do it with a doll or . . . or . . . some such symbol.'

'Yes, sir, of course, sir. That's a much better idea.'

Hugh turned away to hide his laughter and the other boys bit their lips or sniggered into their hands. Peter Holt pulled himself together.

'Sir, will we do how Saint Nicholas gave the money to the old man to save his daughters from selling themselves because he was so poor . . . sir?'

'And tell me, which of you fine, upstanding young fellows is willing to play a girl?' said the Magister.

'Not me!'

'Not likely.'

'What about Hugh?' said Matthew from his place up on the table. 'He has the yellow curls for it. I can think of one of the canons who would dearly love for Hugh to play a girl, and a prostitute at that . . .'

There was a gasp from the boys. As one, they looked at the Magister.

'Matthew, enough.' He brought the cane down hard on the table, his temper at its edge. 'That is enough, I say. These are sacred stories about the benevolence of a saint, a bishop, a father of the Church and a brother in Christ. We have asked His blessing on our work. If you cannot treat it with respect, we shall not do the play at all.'

There was an 'oooh' of disappointment.

'I am serious. Matthew, get down from the table.'

'But . . .'

'Of course I'll play a girl,' said Hugh suddenly, 'then Matthew can throw me a golden purse to save my virtue and my old father' – he took Fitz's arm and his voice shot up an octave – 'my poor old father can sit easy at his hearth till the end of his days.'

With a simper, he twisted one of his curls round a finger. A cheer broke out and a couple of boys clapped.

'But I need two sisters,' said Hugh. 'Who's it to be, then? You've none of you the hair for it, you'd all need a wig.'

Pink and giggling, and with not too much twisting of their arms, a couple of younger boys stumbled forward to play Hugh's sisters. They improvised round the story of the old man forced to sell his daughters for money till Saint Nicholas threw three golden purses through the window of their hovel to save their virtue. Matthew scowled an unsaintly scowl from the table, the wind taken out of his sails. Then all the boys made a makeshift boat from the benches and played out the storm scene with much rolling, pretend sea-sick puking and horribly realistic drowning, till Matthew, recovering his temper and enjoying the sense of power, stilled the storm and brought them safely to shore.

'Now the three soldiers,' called Fitz. 'Let's do the three soldiers.'

Hastily, before there could be more argument, the Magister chose Simon, Peter Holt and Edward

Longnose to play the three soldiers that Saint Nicholas had once saved from hanging. Fitz was to play the executioner with his head in a bag with slits cut out for his eyes.

'Now,' said the Magister. 'Next is the legend of the famine. The people of the country are starving. Matthew, some sacks of corn are unloaded from the ships, but they are not enough, so you will work a miracle . . .'

Several of the boys scrambled up on to the table to play angels carrying corn from heaven. At the moment when they were supposed to bring the sacks down to earth, Matthew gave each of them a none-too-gentle shove on to the floor where they glowered up at him, rubbing their knees.

'There's one more story, sir,' said Matthew.

The Magister turned from talking to the young boys about their wigs. 'Oh?'

'Sir, there's still the cup-bearer.'

'I think we have had enough for today,' said the Magister. 'In fact, we probably have enough altogether. Ours is not the only play to be performed, and the angels flying down from heaven will make a good ending.'

'But, sir,' said Matthew, 'the cup-bearer is important. He served a Jew, didn't he? A heathen. It's the story about the Jew making him blaspheme and Saint Nicholas coming to save the Christian from saying bad words. And we know about the Jews, don't we? I think we should show them for what everyone knows they are, money-lenders . . . heathens . . . drinkers of blood.'

The Magister paused and sucked in his cheeks. He looked round at the expectant boys and glanced up at Matthew.

'Sir, I'm sure my lord Bishop would want that story told, wouldn't he? And so would the Earl.'

It was a statement, not a question. Matthew looked down on the Magister, his jaw set. The Magister thought for a moment longer then gave a curt nod.

'Very well, we will do the story of the cup-bearer immediately before the story of the famine. We will still finish with the angels. It is a good ending. But if we are to do this story, we must pray for guidance that we shall not be tainted with ... with blasphemous, heathenish ways.'

He dropped to his knees and, suddenly serious, the boys did the same. John followed, leaning on a bench to tuck his foot underneath him without keeling over, a troubled frown on his face as he folded his hands and bent his head. The Magister offered up a fervent prayer for deliverance from the ways of pagans and money-lenders, finishing with a Pater Noster.

'Very well,' he said when they were all standing again. 'Fitz, the executioner's part is very small, so you will play the cup-bearer. You are a captive in a Jewish kingdom. You will tell your master the King about Saint Nicholas, how good he is, how benevolent, because of his beliefs, and the King will be angry and try to force you to blaspheme against Christ.'

He crossed himself hurriedly.

'Can you do that?'

'I'll try, sir,' said Fitz, uneasily. 'But will I really have to blaspheme, sir?'

'Nay,' said the Magister. 'Saint Nicholas will come to your rescue. He will carry you up into the clouds before you can say the words.'

'But, sir, Matthew couldn't carry me, not to get up there, let alone on to the dray-cart . . .' Fitz nodded up at the table.

'He will send angels down to fetch you . . . they can lift you somehow between them. We will work out a way . . . that's the least of our difficulties . . .'

Fitz said nothing. He still looked anxious but no more so than the other boys who weren't at all keen to get up on the table again with Matthew.

'Sir,' said Peter Holt, 'who is to play the King?'

There was a pause. Certainly no one would volunteer to play a Jew, King though he might be.

'Peg-leg,' said Matthew with a little smile. 'Peg-leg hasn't had a part yet, not a proper part. He can be the heathen King. He's made for it . . .'

There was silence. The boys grew shifty and looked anywhere but at John. Even the Magister had nothing to say. Quietly, Hugh crossed the room to him, ready to put a hand on his arm.

John took a deep breath. A sudden picture came into his mind of the Jew kneeling at his feet, offering to take him in . . . the society of marked men . . . He pressed his foot into the ground and slowly let out his breath. 'Yes,' he said. 'I'll do that. I'll play the King.'

A quick frown of surprise passed over Matthew's face. He had expected an argument at the least. The boys dragged up the Magister's chair and started to set a bench or two as a banqueting hall.

'Pity we can't have real food,' said Fitz, 'like at the Earl's.'

'You'll have to wait for that,' said Simon. 'You're always thinking of your stomach.'

'Who's talking?'

They were all always thinking of their stomachs. John heaved himself into the Magister's chair and banged on the arm with his fist. The others jumped into their places with Fitz behind John, bearing an imaginary cup in one hand and a jug in the other.

'Like this, sir?' he said to the Magister, miming the pouring out of some wine. The Magister nodded.

'Excellent,' he said. 'Now you must hand it to him. Then I think, John, you must ask a question that leads to your servant telling you about Saint Nicholas. What will you say?'

'I will say,' said John slowly, 'I will say . . .' and he began the scene . . . 'Tell me, young gentile, who was your master before me?'

Fitz hesitated.

'Tell him that you have only one master and that is Christ,' said the Magister, his eyes fixed on John. 'But tell him that you served the blessed Saint Nicholas who has died and is now in heaven with your master.'

He waited for John to act losing his temper, but John merely looked up at him and said softly, 'I see. And you believe this?'

'I do,' said the Magister, still playing the cup-bearer, 'and I believe we should all believe it, sire, even you.'

'Even me?' said John-the-King. 'I am the least likely to believe it, then?'

The Magister pushed Fitz forward but again he hesitated and the Magister spoke for him.

'Sire, you are a Jew.'

'I am, and I have my own beliefs and my own ways, as good as yours, perhaps.'

The boys gathered closer, spellbound, as the discourse grew. John's King did not rage and storm, wave his arms about and froth at the mouth as they had expected. He seemed first genuinely to try to understand, then to become anxious and even afraid of what the cup-bearer was telling him. Then, as his fear grew, he begged and begged the cup-bearer to disown his beliefs till suddenly he banged down his fist again and cried, 'It isn't true. It isn't true. It can't be or everything I have believed is wrong . . . Say it isn't true or . . . or . . .' and he looked up imploringly at the Magister.

Then very quietly he said, 'Well, sir, isn't it time to send in the angels?'

The Magister dropped his head and the atmosphere was broken. Some of the boys started to clap but he held up his hand and cleared his throat.

'If that was acting, John, it was very good acting indeed. Are you sure you have never acted before?'

John shook his head. Was that what acting was? If so, it had all seemed to happen very easily and naturally, so much so, he wasn't sure he could do it again and it came almost as a relief when the Magister went on.

'However, I feel it does not quite tell the story as –

as it should be. I believe it would be better not to play that episode. You played very well . . . but, er, there might be some misunderstanding and, er . . . well . . .' His voice gathered conviction. 'You are, after all, very new here and such a big part . . . and I think we have enough to entertain the crowd without that scene . . .'

His voice faltered again, and he gave John a troubled look.

'You seemed to be . . . sympathetic to the Jew and – to – to ask the audience for sympathy for the Jews in this town would be to ask for trouble, I believe,' he said, 'for – for many reasons. It seemed to me that that was what you . . .' and then almost in a whisper, '. . . they killed Christ, they killed God, John, do you understand that?'

John met his gaze.

The Magister shook his head, straightened up and looked around.

'Come, get down from the table, Matthew. Is it clear, everybody? We go straight from the scene with the execution of the soldiers to the ending with the famine and the angels bringing the corn. Is that clear?'

The boys murmured 'Yes, sir' and started to clear away the benches. John looked at Hugh with a quiet 'phew'. With a smile and a quick shake of his head, Hugh stood behind him and pushed him up out of the Magister's chair. Fitz and Simon dragged the chair back to the top of the long table as Matthew jumped down. He stood in front of John, barring his way.

'Well, that was a pretty performance,' he said quietly, his eyes narrowed. 'Friend of the Jews as well as the devil, are we? I thought as much. I saw you, Peg-leg. I've seen you talking to Reuben ben Ezra. Oh don't try and look puzzled, your acting's not that good.'

'Reuben ben Ezra, is it? I didn't know his name, that's all.'

'Tcha . . . you sicken me. You sicken me with your claw foot and your devil worship and your love of the Jews. You should be . . . you should . . .'

'Yes?'

But the Magister took Matthew's shoulder and steered him away and John and Hugh went outside.

'He surely hates me,' said John.

'He's afraid of you. And the more you keep calm and don't let him wind you up, the more he hates you. He hates me too, but at least it's because I'm Boy Bishop and that's what he wanted for himself. With you it's all in his head.'

'My foot's real.'

'Yes, but what he thinks of it isn't. The devil and all that.'

'Doesn't everyone believe in the devil?'

'Of course, but not living in your foot,' said Hugh with a laugh. 'He has better places to hide.'

'That's true,' thought John, 'if he exists at all.'

They wandered down between the market stalls in silence, making for the cathedral doors, a thin film of snow beginning to cover the ground in the fading light. A flight of crows flew over, squabbling and cawing and landing on the heads of the stone kings high over the doors. John clapped his hands and the echo made them lift into the air again like black rags and they flapped off towards the rising moon. John gave his little ploughman a pat, Hugh opened the small door and they went in. Matthew wouldn't follow them there, or if he did, he wouldn't pick a quarrel in case any of the canons saw him.

Inside, in the glow of the candles, the pilgrims continued their shuffling around the arcade and the pedlars and the men of business stood about in the nave, but the bustle had quietened at the end of the day. There was no sign of Reuben ben Ezra but the pedlar that Hugh had seen in the woods was still selling his bones to the imprudent, but in a desultory way.

Suddenly, there was a stir as Canon Senan strode out of the vestry between the columns, seeming to bring a blast of cold air with him in spite of his scarlet robe. He stood for a moment glaring round him, then he caught sight of the pedlar, made straight for him and took him by the scruff of the neck. For a moment the man clawed at the Canon's hand, whining and grovelling, but without a word, the Canon hustled him down the nave and out through the door. Around him, everything went still. People stared open-mouthed; fingers froze in the middle of telling their beads; voices hushed in mid-sentence. The Canon slammed the door and, with a disdainful look on his gaunt face, brushed off his hands and disappeared into the vestry, slamming that door too. After a moment, like a picture coming to life, people recovered themselves, returning to their devotions or other affairs, some nodding in approval at the Canon's action, but some of them still staring at the vestry door, a question on their faces.

'Well,' said Hugh, his eyebrows raised, 'what was all that about, d'you suppose?'

John shrugged. They squatted on the base of a column, their backs against it. John's scars were beginning to heal and they itched. He scratched himself gently against the stone. 'Perhaps he knows about the bones.'

'Sssh,' said Hugh with a laugh and looking round. 'That pedlar's not the only one, I'll bet. Can't be just that, surely. And I bet the canons know about it; they probably take a cut.'

'Not Canon Senan. He may be a monster when it comes to a beating, but he's honest.'

'Perhaps not him then, but some of them.'

'They're supposed to be men of God.'

'Men, yes . . . of God? Hmm.'

Hugh looked distant for a moment. John hesitated. 'Was it – was it true?' he said.

'Was what true?'

'About . . . about what Matthew said. About you . . . and the Canon who . . .'

Hugh gave a little smile and lifted his chin. 'He just looks . . . so far. And he can look all he likes but he won't catch me. Don't worry, Peg. I can look out for myself.'

'Shouldn't you say something . . . ?'

'It would be my word against his. When – if – he looks at others – that way . . . or touches them . . . then I'll do something. Don't worry.'

John closed his eyes for a moment, shaking his head, then looked up at the angels. What was the use of making beautiful buildings, or angels and kings and ploughmen to put in them, for men like that ... or like Canon Humphrey and Canon Senan and even the Magister who had left him to be beaten till he bled. Once he had loved the cathedral and all that was in it but that was before ... before he had become too close to what men could do within it. But that wasn't the cathedral's fault, nor the fault of those who made it ...

Hugh followed his eyes. 'They've got their work cut out, those angels ... Peg, I know what you're thinking, but they're a long way away. They take a lot of reaching up there in their heaven. It's hard for anyone to try and get to them.'

'Yes, I know,' said John with a sigh, lowering his head.

Instantly, Hugh's face crumpled and he struck a hand to his forehead. 'I'm sorry, I'm sorry, Peg. I was forgetting ...'

'Nay,' said John. 'It's just that ... My father and the others, they put them up there so people would know what heaven would be like. That it was a place worth aiming for. It doesn't work, does it?'

'Not for some, Peg. But for others it does. It must. Look at them.'

They gazed up at the tiny gold stars streaming across the distant ceiling and the angels, smiling and radiant, holding their garlands, playing their music. Hugh smiled too, looking for all the world like one of them.

'It must. You can practically hear them. And it worked for your father, didn't it?'

'Do you really suppose that's where . . . ?'

'Where else?' said Hugh. 'He made the angels, didn't he?'

But stone angels, however bright with gold, were but small comfort. After a few moments, Hugh saw he would have to try again.

'Well, you helped to make them, so if anyone understands, you do.'

'Sort of.' John's reply was grudging. 'I used to before . . . I really believed before it all got taken away.'

'All?'

'Everything. That's how it seems.'

'I know . . . I know what you've lost. But not them. You could make them again, more angels, somewhere else, some day . . .'

John shook his head. 'How? Getting to be an apprentice is difficult. It stays in the family. And most of the masons are gone now, the ones that knew me, that might have taken me on. They go from building to building, where they're needed. I saw the last one leave the other day, going to Norway to the new cathedral there.'

'Didn't you ask to go with him?'

'I should have, I suppose, but it's too late now . . . he was in a hurry and oh . . .' John sighed. 'He wasn't one I knew all that well . . . I . . . Hugh, most what I want . . . I want to find my father's tools – then I'd feel . . . well, part of it again maybe. He made them. They were . . . He was showing me how . . .'

'Where are they?'

John shrugged. He began picking at the hem of his gown.

'Well, where do you think?'

'Magnus said the master mason may have them.'

'Go and see. Ask him. Why not?'

'He's . . . he's . . . well, it would be like you going to see my lord Bishop.'

Hugh pulled a face. 'It's worth a try though, isn't it?'

John bent down to rub his foot, his head almost on his knee, then he stood up and stretched, and as he did so, he seemed to catch the eye of his angel, the last angel, the angel that had fallen. He let drop his arms, still looking upwards. It seemed as if the lute it held was pointing straight towards him, as if the angel was about to toss it into his hands. For an instant, he wanted to reach out and catch it. He smiled and the moment was gone. He rubbed his face hard with his knuckles, screwing up his eyes, suddenly feeling a long-forgotten happiness bubble up inside him.

He looked at Hugh.

'I reckon so,' he said. 'I reckon so . . . it's worth a try.'

Chapter 8

The masons' yard was locked. John's face fell. The masons' yard used always to be open. If it was locked, maybe it meant the master had gone away too.

'You could try up in the roof at the crossing over the choir. 'E do go up there sometimes,' said an old man sweeping up a few dead leaves round the outside of the yard. He was bent double, a dribble hanging from his red, wrinkled nose, his fingers gnarled and frozen round the broom handle.

'Let's go and see,' said John to Hugh, brightening up.

'Not likely,' said Hugh. 'Up there? With the bats and the spooks and Saint Hugh knows what?'

'Don't be a wimp,' said John, with a laugh. 'It's magic up there. You can toboggan down the floors over the vaults on your arse, it's so steep in some places.'

He hurried into the cathedral, Hugh tagging along behind.

'You need a light or it's dangerous. If you slip, you could lie at the bottom of the really steep bits till the next time someone comes up, and that could be when you're bones.'

'De-lightful,' said Hugh. 'Rather you than me. Why don't you wait till the master comes down? You know what happened last time you went up somewhere they thought you shouldn't be.'

John rubbed his back. It was still sore in places but mending quite fast now. 'Mmm,' he said, 'but this is in the roof over the choir, miles from the west front where I was before. No one can see you up there and even the door is hard to find. Look there it is, hidden in the wall by the column ... I bet you've never noticed it before.'

Hugh shook his head. John whipped a candle from its holder in a side chapel and then took another, unlit, for luck.

'Go on, why don't you come? You've got Saint Hugh *and* Saint Nicholas now, they'll both take care of you.'

But Hugh shook his head again. Not that he wasn't on pretty good terms with the saints, but he'd rather not risk it, not with Saint Nicholas' Day so near. He touched John's arm. 'Couldn't it wait till he comes down?' he said.

'Well ...' said John, reluctantly. 'He might be ages if it's a big job he's doing. Hugh ... I really want ... If I could only have ...'

Hugh gave a little smile and nodded.

'I won't be long. Quick as I can,' said John, eagerly.

'All right. I'll wait here.'

Hugh stood guard as John slipped inside the tiny door hidden in the shadows.

'Won't be long' was going to be an understatement of some magnitude. The stairs wound up and up and he had to stop several times to ease his foot. The candle guttered in the draught and the wax dripped on his hand till he tipped it forward and it fell on to the grey stone slabs of the stairs. In places, a rope trailed up the inside wall like a creeping plant, giving a handhold. He used it to haul himself up, but when the rope came to an end, John found himself almost crawling upwards, his foot dragging.

'Can't be much further,' he said to himself. 'I don't remember it being this far.'

Suddenly the stairs stopped and gave on to a ledge. He raised the candle high. Shadows shifted and hovered round the huge cavern-like space and dissolved into darkness. Below and above him, gigantic beams were hammered into one another as if they would last till doomsday, a huge web of timber against the rubble and brick of the walls. A rickety wooden platform led away into the void in front of him and on either side deep pits dropped away steeply, echoing the arches of the vaults below. Hanging on to a beam, he leant over, gingerly, the light of the candle just reaching as far as the bottom. It was a long, long way down and the smooth sides of the pit offered no handhold to get back. Suddenly, tobogganing didn't seem like so much fun. He pulled himself upright and crept forward a few paces along the platform, catching his foot in a loose board that clanked back into place with a sound that seemed it would wake the dead.

The dead. Ghosts. That wasn't such a good thought, either. He paused. All that was nonsense, just like the devil, stupid stories that pillocks like

Matthew believed. Stories people told you to scare you into making you behave the way they wanted you to. Wasn't it? But if you thought about it, people supposed to know about such things, like the Magister and the canons and even the Bishop maybe . . . they believed too. But, he decided firmly, not him.

He shuffled forward, his foot hurting where the loose board had scuffed it. If the master mason was working up here somewhere, surely he would see a light. But the crossing was some way ahead, and if the master was a long way down one of the transepts, a light might not show. A few steps further and he thought, 'But I would hear something, wouldn't I? I'd either hear or see something . . . hammering, or the saw on the stone. There's no one here. No one but me . . .'

Suddenly, something brushed his cheek. Only a cobweb but it was enough. He spun round and his foot gave out. He slipped and the candle died. Darkness came down on him like the wing of a bat folding across his eyes. The candle rolled, then rattled down, down into the pit at the side of the platform. It stopped, and the silence that followed it was enormous. He lay quite still so as not to hear the sound of his own breathing.

Nothing. Nothing to see, nothing to hear . . . it was as if all his senses had deserted him. Well, he must do something. Gradually he hunched his shoulders up to his ears, easing them, and looked around. Not even a pin-prick of light to help him. He would have to feel his way. Putting a hand forward cautiously, he began to inch forward. He dared not stand up. If he lost his balance in the dark, the pits were waiting, their gaping maws open to swallow him. The wooden platform was narrow, but he hadn't come in too far and if he felt around him on either side he would know where the edge was. Of course he would.

Just as he felt he must be nearing the end of the platform, close to the ledge, another cobweb caught him and he wheeled round. His foot slipped and off came his clog. He groped about wildly, but knocked against it and only succeeded in jerking it over the edge to join the candle-end in the pit below. He reached after it, but drew his hand back quickly in case . . . in case . . . suppose a hand came up out of the dark to meet his own? He jammed his hands under his armpits. The loud clatter of the falling clog seemed endless. Surely the whole of the cathedral below could hear it. But this place was like a tomb, vast and echoing – and remote. The outside world did not exist up here.

His clog was gone. Now he would be in trouble. He sat up and wiped his nose on his sleeve, cursing himself for his stupidity. He should have realized the old man with the broom didn't know what he was talking about. He should have seen at once that the master mason wasn't up here and gone straight down again. Hugh was right, he shouldn't have come at all. At least Hugh would be waiting for him. He turned on to his knees and stopped.

Which way was he facing? Where was the doorway? For a moment, blind panic overtook him.

The doorway could be anywhere. What if he went the wrong way, on and on the length of the vaults over the choir? And when he got to the crossing, which way then? He would never get out. He would end up in one of the pits. Taking deep breaths, he told himself this was rubbish too, just like the ghosts, just like ... just like ... No. If he got to the crossing he would know he simply had to turn back the way he had come, no matter how long it took.

He tried a prayer, but who should he pray to? The God that had taken his father and his foot and his future? What use would that be? His foot was throbbing. His foot ... wait a minute ... under his foot, somewhere directly beneath him were the angels, his angel. He was up here, sitting on the angel's back. The angel wouldn't let him be lost again. The angel would carry him back into the world. He laughed aloud and the sound came back to him, over and over and over.

Calming down, he made himself think back.

'Angel? Listen ... How many times did I turn to grab at the clog before it fell? Once, twice ... Then I sat up ... but which way was I facing then?'

He thought again. Once, twice ... That was it ...

He scrambled forward, feeling for the end of the platform and the beginning of the rubble and stone by the wall. There it was! With a shout he pulled himself upright. He was a few moments finding the opening to the stair when he turned and hurled the second candle into space. He heard it spin and ricochet down into the pit.

'Thank you, angel,' he whispered aloud, and with

another laugh and a clap of his hands that echoed round and round again, he turned his back on the darkness, sat down on the top step and bumped his way down the stairs. Behind him he could hear the word 'angel, angel, angel' fainter and fainter in the dark. Half-falling, half-sliding he careered down the spiral of the stairs, banging against the walls, his single clog clattering. He burst out of the door at the bottom to find Hugh, biting his nails with worry and, for Hugh, looking extremely angry.

'Sweet Jesu, where have you been? Do you know how long you were up there?'

'I – I—'

'I didn't know what to do. I couldn't have hung round much longer, people were beginning to look and I didn't know what had happened to you. Peg, I was getting really worried. What on earth have you been doing?' His voice rose to a squeak.

'I'm sorry, I'm sorry,' said John. 'I got sort of lost, I couldn't tell which way . . . Anyway, I'm all right.'

'Lost?' Hugh put his hands to his head.

'The candle went out. I didn't know which way I was going.'

Hugh spun away, then turned back. 'You're not safe to be out alone, you aren't.'

'I know. I'm sorry.'

'Huh.'

'I am, I'm really sorry. It's just as well you didn't come. You would *not* have liked it.'

'Nor did you, did you? *Did* you?'

John gave a sheepish grin. 'Not much, no. It was different when we all used to be up there together –

you know, all the masons. Voices. Lots more light. Lamps, not just a candle. Different.'

'Oh well,' said Hugh, calming down, 'perhaps you won't go off like that again in a hurry.'

He didn't wait for an answer since it might not be what he wanted to hear.

'Anyway,' he said, 'did you find him?'

'No,' said John, 'he wasn't up there. When I saw the yard locked up I should have known. That old man must have been, I don't know, thinking about some other time, I suppose.'

They set off down into the nave. As they passed under the last angel, John looked up and winked. Hugh didn't notice; he was looking down at John's foot.

'What's wrong? You're limping?'

'I always limp, remember?'

'Not like that. You're like a ship in a gale, heave ho, heave ho.' He gave a rolling imitation.

'Thanks a lot. If you must know, I lost a clog up there.'

'You'll be in trouble.'

'Tell me something I don't know.'

He took off his remaining clog and dangled it from a finger.

'Your feet'll freeze like that.'

'What else am I supposed to do?'

They chuntered on, bickering amicably, till outside the cathedral, they turned towards the schoolhouse. Fitz was loping towards them between the market stalls.

'Come on, you two, it's the last practice before

tomorrow. We've been looking for you everywhere. The Magister's going mad in there.'

They broke into a run, slipping and sliding over the icy stones, and disappeared into the school-house.

Chapter 9

The stars were still out as, for once, the boys leapt out of bed, broke the ice and gave their faces a hasty smear, tumbled down the stairs, shuffled on their clogs and staggered out into the freezing air. The Feast of Fools had come.

The great cathedral bell tolled mightily as they scuttled across to the vestry where the Magister waited, cane in hand, but with what might almost have been a twinkle in his eye. He rounded them up, counted them and shepherded them outside the west door, where a dray was already set up for the plays.

The night before, John had found an old, abandoned pair of clogs half-buried in the straw at the end of the hall beneath the dormitory. They were a bit tight, but they would do, and more important, no one would notice that his own had disappeared.

The whole of the square still sparkled with frost. Tumblers and stilt walkers jostled jugglers and fire-eaters. Performing dogs barked and whined and a huge grizzly bear growled and pawed the air on the end of its stout chain. The red robes of the clerics, glowing in the last of the moonlight, looked cheery and warm but the boys' teeth chattered as they jigged up and down, chafing their hands and bumping into each other in excitement. Rufus came worming through the growing crowd to find them.

'You coming too?' said Hugh.

'They do let me out this day in the year. Hey, 'ow is it?' he said to John.

'Better. I can sit down now.'

Rufus nodded and grinned. 'Worse than the Harrowing of Hell,' he said. 'Wait till you see my guv'nor as the devil.'

'The devil?'

'Harrowing of Hell. Cooks' Guild's doin' the play later. My guv'nor's Satan.'

John laughed. 'He's not that bad, is he?'

'Some days,' said Rufus, with a shrug. 'Others he's too pissed to bother. My arse is often black and blue – but not like that ... like what the Canon did to you.'

He shook his head, his face serious for once, but not for long. He broke into a grin. 'Never mind,' he said. 'It's today now, and it's gonna be a good'un.'

He peered over the steep path down the escarpment. Way below, the city was stirring. Shutters were opening and lamps lit. At the end of the main street, the baker's door had been flung wide and inside, the oven roared. John thought he could smell the baking from here. A man passed by calling his wares, roasted chickens impaled on a rod slung over his shoulder. Hot grease was dripping down and sizzling on the stones. The boys' stomachs growled their lack of money.

'Don't you worry,' said Rufus, searching round

under his clothes. He produced a few ancient bits of bread and cheese and shared them round.

'Oh, yes please,' said Fitz. 'That'll last us a while.'

'There's no one in any of the canons' kitchens today,' said Simon, gnawing at a dry lump of cheese, 'can you believe it? But we'll be able to beg a bit, here and there, I suppose . . .'

'We shan't get much,' said Hugh. 'Everyone knows it's our turn tomorrow, on Saint Nicholas' Day.'

'We can give them a hard time then, though,' said Fitz. 'We'll still be full to busting from the Earl's feast but there's always room for more and we can get their money . . . lovely money . . .'

He hunched his shoulders and smacked his hands together, chomping on his stale crust, crumbs tumbling down his chest. Round them the performers practised a few tricks, warming themselves up till they should reach the people down in the city where the real money was. Then they'd really let themselves go. A stilt walker ran up and, straddling his legs wide, passed straight over Rufus's head.

'Phhaw,' he said, 'wouldn't like to get stuck under there,' and he wrinkled up his nose and flapped his hand in front of his face. The boys grinned. Rufus would be good for a laugh all day.

A sudden joyful peal of beals rang out from the cathedral and the Lord of Misrule bounded on to the dray. He capered about in his black and yellow motley, his cap bells jingling. Turning a somersault in the air, he leapt down, laying about him with his pig's bladder at any head or backside he could reach.

With a great cheer, heard and answered from the city below, the procession sprang to life.

Running alongside the parade, dodging the pig's bladder, the boys set off towards the path. As it tipped over the edge of the escarpment they pelted downwards, faster and faster, unable to stop until they rolled and tumbled in the crisp, wintry grass. John started with them, but lost his balance and grabbed the railing. He came on more slowly, holding on hand-over-hand, so his foot wouldn't give way under the strain of the steep descent. With a pang, he watched the others go ahead without him. He would have to catch them up at the bottom. Hugh at least would wait for him there.

Halfway down he passed the Jew's house. The shutters were closed and no smoke came from the chimney. It seemed almost deserted but the Star of David still hung over the door, glinting a little in the first light of dawn. A small stream, frozen at the edges, splashed over the rocks of a small precipice into the garden directly behind the house, then plunged down out of sight, into the forbidden places where the houses of the other Jews were.

Behind him, John heard a sound that jarred amongst the laughing and bustle. He looked round in time to see a gobbet of spittle hit the ground in front of the door. Someone gave a low, mocking cheer. Whether it was one of the men or one of the canons he couldn't tell but several of them were glancing at the Jew's house and crossing themselves, or hurrying to get by quickly, their heads averted as if they were afraid. He heard the words 'devil' and 'heathen' bandied about and another man mimed cutting his throat with his finger, then pointed it at the house as he passed it.

Further back, he saw the round, pink head of Canon Gwyllim bouncing up and down among the crowd, leaning backwards to stop himself staggering out of control down the slope. At his side were the grizzled locks of Canon Humphrey bursting out of a bonnet tied tightly under his chin. As they came closer, they eyed each other, then the Jew's house, crossed themselves and edged away to the far side of the path.

John hurried to catch up with Hugh, but his foot wouldn't let him. Then he had the bright idea of hoisting himself up on the railing and sliding down on his stomach. He came down so fast that, without losing momentum, he reeled across the gaps, grabbed the next bit and whizzed on. At the bottom, with a yell, he shot into the air. Hugh and Rufus took the brunt as he landed and they all piled into a heap on the ground. As they untangled themselves, Hugh grabbed the railing.

'Hey, that's a good way . . . let's go back up.'

'Don't be daft. Time enough when we've got to go back up. We're not going up there again now,' said Fitz. 'Come on, let's go . . .'

John held Hugh back and jerked his head back towards the Jew's house.

'Why do they spit? Why are they afraid of him?'

'What?'

'They spat at the Jew's house . . .'

'What? Oh, Peg, don't bother with that now.'

'I know they think the Jews killed . . . you know . . . but that's old history now. Isn't it?'

'Try telling them that. They owe him money, stupid. What do you think?' said Rufus.

John shrugged. 'Well, I suppose so,' he said, unconvinced. Owing money seemed no better reason for spitting at people than old history.

The procession weaved around the city, sometimes parting to flow down two narrow streets and meeting up again where the streets joined. John saw people laugh and clap and shout as they hung out of windows overhanging the cobbles, or perched along the crooked walls. As the rich men at the west end of the main street flung money, poor men tried to catch it before the acrobats could reach it. Young women waved their aprons; babes in arms chuckled and bobbed up and down; apprentice lads whistled and cat-called, everyone in high good humour except one old crone who emptied her piss-pot on the parade and sent everyone scattering. The boys grabbed at tankards of ale and bladders of wine as they passed from hand to hand. The noise was deafening.

In the main square the procession stopped and the proper show began. The Lord of Misrule attacked the crowd with the pig's bladder, tipping off hats, lifting skirts, banging noses. John and Hugh hauled themselves up on a window sill to watch the performing dogs tottering along on their hind legs, their necks in bright coloured ruffles. They roly-polyed over, their legs in the air; they jumped through hoops. The stilt walkers held a mock battle, throwing bags of flour that burst and showered everyone in sticky powder, and the acrobats tumbled and flew through the air to oohs and aahs from the crowd. There were gasps as the fire-eater knelt and held his flame up high, opening his mouth so wide the boys thought they could see down into his belly. John and Hugh nudged each other when, slowly, he pushed the torch lower and lower down his throat, then pulled it out, the flame gone.

'Fire must still be in his belly,' said one old woman. ' 'S right, ma,' came an answer, 'he can roast 'is own dinner in there,' and the old lady's eyes widened. The fire-eater jumped up with a triumphant shout. He bowed and hurried to pass round his hat. John grinned as Rufus leapt forward, tossed in a crust and got a clip round the ear for his pains.

The square was seething with revellers. More and more pushed in till they could scarcely move. When the grizzly bear lumbered into the middle, those at the front recoiled. John and Hugh heaved their legs up out of the way of the crush. Those at the back were crammed against the walls and started to push forward. Young lads prodded and poked at the great animal till it roared and pawed the air, and there were shrieks and hoots and cries. Again the crowd drew back and then surged forward and the bear's claw caught one man on the shoulder, tearing his tunic. Ale and wine were running freely and tempers beginning to fray.

'Boys!' yelled the Magister. 'Come away.'

John and Hugh scrambled down and pushed their way towards him. The man with the torn tunic and the owner of the bear were fighting now and tussles were breaking out all over. A few people began to squeeze their way through to the road that led to the path up the hill.

'We must get back and be ready for the play,' said the Magister, pushing and pulling them through the hordes. At the foot of the hill he stopped and counted them all again.

'Come,' he said, 'it may not be safe down here from now on. Those that want to see the plays will sober up on the climb back to God's house, but the rest . . . We will go now while we can.'

He started the long haul up the escarpment, pausing every now and then for breath. Some of the boys flung themselves down in the grass at the side of the path, damp now that the early winter sun was melting the frost.

'No time for that,' said the Magister, giving them a sharp prod with the cane. 'You can rest at the top.'

They crawled on up the hill. Suddenly, John stopped.

'Where's Rufus?' he said.

'Never mind him,' said Hugh, 'he can look after himself. And his guv'nor was still down there. Didn't you see him knocking back the ale? He can't be too bothered about his play.'

John looked back. As he watched, the crowd ebbed and flowed, making wide ripples across the square and through the streets like an invading ocean. To make out Rufus from up here, or even the fat cook with his enormous belly, was impossible, no matter how hard he tried. The fight around the bear was a tight, black, heaving knot. A few more figures were beginning to toil up the hill, but they were far below him still. He turned to find the Magister and the boys already ahead of him. He began to climb again, trying to hurry, but his foot didn't like the hill and he found himself slowing down, limping and stumbling.

At the gate of the Jew's house, he paused. In the frost still coating the path in the shade of the porch, a patch had been wiped clean where the gobbet of spittle had been.

'Clean now,' he thought, 'but why should they have to clear it up at all?'

As he stood there, he thought he saw a shutter move. A pair of dark eyes was watching him through the gap. He went a little nearer. For a moment he stared back, then, glancing up the path towards the backs of the other boys still labouring up the hill, he went in through the gate and almost up to the window.

'H-hello,' he said. The eyes didn't move. Had he been heard? The eyes were regarding him very gravely. They sat in a pale, solemn face, framed with tight black curls under a small version of the Jew's hat.

'Hello,' said John again. No reply. Suddenly, John realized that this house had glass in the windows, like the windows in the cathedral. The Jew was really rich then. Is that how you got rich, lending money? Surely not if you were never paid back like Hugh had said. But glass . . .

Of course! Whoever it was couldn't hear him through the glass. John raised his hand slowly to the pale face at the window. After a moment, whoever it was raised a hand in return and a hesitant smile broke out beneath the dark eyes. Then the shutter closed quickly. John was about to move away, when the door of the house opened a crack and the face peered through.

'Hello,' said John.

A boy about his own age, but a little smaller, edged through the door, leaving it open a crack behind him. His clothes were much like John's only brown, but on his arm was a yellow badge.

'Hello,' he said, solemnly. 'Shalom aleikhem.'

'What does that mean?' said John.

'It means peace,' said the boy. 'It means peace be with you.'

John liked that.

'Sha – sha – whatever you said, to you too,' he said. The boy smiled.

'Shalom,' he said. 'What is your name? Mine is Aaron.'

'Like in the Bible story? I thought . . .'

'Of course,' said the boy, 'they were our stories first, didn't you know? What is your name?'

'John. Some people call me Peg.'

'Peg?'

John shifted a little on his foot and Aaron looked down.

'Peg-leg,' said John, with a rueful smile.

'Oh, your leg,' he said, a sudden light in his eyes, 'yes, my father told me. You are the one he found. The one who was beaten so hard by the – the Canon. Is that what you call him?'

'Yes. But I'm all right now. Beating's beating and you get better. My foot is mine, it's like this for ever.'

Aaron nodded seriously. 'My father said—' but a woman's voice came from inside the house and Aaron slipped back inside, holding the door open. 'He said you were brave, but that you were a marked man too, like – like us . . .'

The voice came again. Aaron called out in Hebrew then grinned at John. 'Good-bye . . . Peg,' he said. With a nod, he tapped his yellow badge, raised a finger, disappeared inside and closed the door.

'Sha – shalom . . .' said John, for some reason more than a little saddened that the boy had gone. His spirit seemed to sink with his going. He came out of the gate. Coming up towards him were more and more people climbing the hill, panting and complaining, red and sweating. As they passed him they glanced at the Jew's house, then gave him a suspicious look, crossed themselves and, breathless though they were, hurried past. John caught hold of the railing and began to heave himself onwards. At the top he looked back, but Aaron's house was shuttered and seemingly in darkness.

Across the square, framed in the arches of the west doors, stood the dray. A short ladder was set up at one end for easy mounting, and a rough canopy covered the top. From high above, the stone kings and saints seemed to look down with restrained curiosity and lower down, a tall figure of Christ stretched his arms out wide to welcome the players and the audience alike. The crowd was beginning to gather round. Rufus raced past John, giving him a friendly thump on the shoulder as he went.

'Come on, ye old tortoise, yer ain't that slow, are ye?'

The cook wheezed up, his eyes bulging fit to burst. 'God's bones, that hill's enough to kill ye. Thank Saint Aelred it's only once a year . . .' and he tottered on, coughing and spluttering, his face the colour of raw beef.

John followed him and slid in amongst the other boys before the Magister could miss him. Their play was to come after the scriveners' play about Christ arguing with the priests in the temple, and before the cooks' Harrowing of Hell.

Whistles and cheers broke out as the goldsmiths' company, resplendent in gorgeous robes and golden crowns, prepared to play the story of the three Magi.

'Is it real gold, d'you think?' said Hugh in a whisper.

'Not right through,' said John, 'not solid gold, but those crowns are gilded with thin gold you can bet your life. Like the angels. Nothing shines like real gold. It's gold leaf, I'd wager on it.'

Rufus blew out his cheeks. 'Think I'll grow up to be a goldsmith then,' he said.

'No,' said Fitz, with much feeling, 'I'd stick with food if I were you.'

'If you've got that kind of money you can buy all the food you want,' said Simon, his stomach rumbling.

'Shut up about food,' said Hugh. 'I'm starving.'

'Da-daaah!'

Rufus searched about in his clothes again and

triumphantly produced a bruised-looking apple and some grey, flattened pastry. Instantly, a clutch of hands reached out to grab them.

'Wait a minute, wait for it,' he said, snatching them back. 'Share and share alike, gents. I got 'em' – he looked round with a wink – 'and I'll give 'em out.'

By the time he had divided up the pastry it was little more than crumbs but he handed the apple to each boy in turn, everyone watching carefully to see that the bites were exactly fair.

Suddenly a drum began to beat and the crowd turned towards the dray with a babble of excitement. One of the goldsmiths' company jumped up and blew a blast on a shiny, curled horn that echoed round and round the square. The boys put their fingers in their ears but it summoned everyone, even the poor soul at the edge of the square having a tooth drawn with pincers by a grubby quack doctor, to the amusement of the bystanders. With white knuckles, he gripped the arms of a makeshift chair till, with a final bellow, he gave up his molar. To groans from the onlookers, especially the boys, the quack waved it in the air, and, mopping at the blood dribbling at his mouth with a filthy rag, the man tottered over to the dray, ready for the play to begin.

The Visit of the Magi was full of pomp and ceremony.

'Look,' said John in a whisper to Hugh, 'you're not the only one.'

The Virgin Mary holding her baby under the canopy was a young apprentice with mutinous blue eyes and a white veil. He held his doll-baby awkwardly and, throughout the proceedings, looked as if he wished the floor of the dray would open and he could drop through. But the kings took their time to deliver their gifts, making long, pompous speeches before they bowed graciously and took their leave.

'Boys!'

The Magister hissed at them through the crowd and beckoned them urgently. 'No time for standing about gawping at all that,' he said. 'It's time to get ready.'

They congregated outside the vestry door, where Matthew was waiting, already dressed as Saint Nicholas, in a cope and mitre, carrying his bishop's crook. John suddenly realized that he hadn't been with them down in the city, at least he hadn't seen him, and he wondered why. But this wasn't a moment for asking questions.

They foraged among the pile of odd garments, soldierly-looking helmets and swords, angels' robes and feather-covered, leather wings. Hugh lifted up his woman's gown.

'Hmm,' he said, 'not too sure about this.'

'All right for you,' said one of the younger boys, struggling into his gown, 'at least you haven't got to wear *this* . . .' and he held up a wig of manky horsehair covered with a wimple. He put it on to shrieks of laughter from the others, till he lashed out with his fists and the Magister stopped him with a tap of the cane.

'Remember,' he said, as sternly as ever, 'we are here to teach the ungodly the ways of Christ Jesus revealed through our beloved Saint Nicholas, the patron saint of all children ... including you, for your sins,' and he made Matthew lead them in repeating 'Christ's cross be my speed and Saint Nicholas' over and over till it was their turn to mount the stage.

Chapter 10

Boos and catcalls from the crowd put a stop to the scriveners' play. Whatever the elders in the temple had to say to the boy Jesus, the mob didn't want to know.

'Get a shift on, we ain't got all day,' came a cry.

'Aye! Get off! You're boring the arse off us!' came another.

The boys looked at the Magister, their faces anxious.

'The arguments are above their heads. They are ignorant animals,' he said. 'Our stories will please them more. Play as well as you have in the schoolhouse and all will be well. You will see.'

The boys nodded, looking hardly less worried than before.

'They can boo all they like,' said Matthew, setting his jaw. 'They won't stop me. Come on.'

For once, the set of Matthew's jaw came as a call to arms. The boys processed up to the dray and waited for the unfortunate elders to come tumbling down, missing the ladder in their haste, spattered with mud and rotten fruit and worse.

'You're welcome to it,' said one of them as he

wiped his face on the tail of his gown. 'You won't catch me back there in a hurry.'

Matthew mounted the ladder. He caught his foot in his cope and stumbled on to the stage. He looked furious, but his entrance brought a cheer from the crowd. He looked daggers at them, but straightened himself out, drew a deep breath and addressed them.

'I am Saint Nicholas.'

'Oh ah,' yelled a voice. 'Tell us another one.'

But the crowd made shushing noises, and another voice shouted, 'Give 'im a chance. 'E's only a bit of a lad.'

'I am Saint Nicholas,' said Matthew again, 'come to tell you my story to help Christ Jesus save you from your sins.'

'Woooah,' went the crowd.

'Just as well we aren't going to do the baby Saint Nicholas and his mother's milk,' thought John. Unperturbed, Matthew went on and introduced the play. The crowd settled down and began to listen.

Frightened of missing his entrance, an agitated Edward Longnose kept whispering 'Is it now?' to the Magister. The Magister kept shushing him, but at last the moment came. The Magister gave the supporting frame of the canopy a shake and three loops of rope dropped down into view to an 'ooooh' from the crowd. Edward, Simon and Peter Holt, their hands held out in front of them as if they were tied at the wrist, mounted the ladder. Heads bowed, they each stood under a noose, waiting.

'What you bin and done then, lads?' called the joker in the crowd.

'Wouldn't you like to know, saucy,' answered a woman's raucous voice and the crowd went wild.

'They are traitors!'

Fitz had to call out his line several times from under his hood before they heard him and quietened down.

'They are traitors to the King and deserve to die.'

The crowd murmured its assent with enthusiasm. Traitors might well deserve a pelting. Hastily, Edward Longnose stepped forward to testify.

'I've an aged mother at home to care for. What would happen to her if I should die?'

'Aaah,' went the crowd, holding back their missiles.

The other two soldiers gave testimony, but Fitz would have none of it. His hood was giving him trouble. He held on to it with one hand so he could see out of the slits, and shoved each head in its noose with the other. John agonized for him as he watched him get well and truly tangled up.

'Come up and give yer a 'and, shall I?' called the joker.

The crowd roared. Fitz untangled himself and got ready to mime the moment of pulling the rope to have the three soldiers dangling.

'Go-ee!' yelled the crowd.

Matthew raised Saint Nicholas' crozier.

'Thou shalt not die,' he cried. 'I release you in the name of Christ Jesus.'

Behind the canopy, the Magister pulled on a hidden rope, the nooses vanished upwards and the three soldiers lifted their hands, released from their bonds.

The crowd cheered. They cheered the rescue from the sinking ship even louder, making sea-sick noises and drowning glugs with great gusto all the way through the scene. Then it was Hugh's turn. Pale and nervous he turned to John.

'Wish me luck, Peg,' he whispered, a desperate look on his face. John, still sweating from the shipwreck, crossed his fingers. Fitz took up his place as the old father, and Hugh tripped lightly up the ladder, holding up his skirts, his 'sisters' stumbling up behind him.

'Father dear,' said Hugh, falsetto, and the crowd whooped and whistled.

'Father dear, we are so poor,' Hugh tried again.

His 'sisters' nodded vigorously, their wigs wobbling and slipping over their eyes.

'What shall we do, what shall we do?'

'Come 'ome with me an' I'll tell yer,' screeched the raucous woman. The crowd roared but suddenly everything went quiet. Heads turned away from the dray and there was a gasp. Cutting a swathe through the crush came Canon Senan, his face contorted and scarlet with rage, a three-thonged scourge in his hand. He lay about him, snarling and grunting with the effort, the scourge whining through the air and lashing down as the crowd scattered, trying to get away from the cutting blows. People held their heads, their cheeks or their hands where the scourge caught them, the blood beginning to well up. Like an avenging angel he came through the throng till he arrived at the foot of the dray.

'Get down,' he said, his voice low and shaking

with fury, glaring at Hugh. 'Come down from there you – you . . . blasphemy, blasphemy . . .'

He leapt on to the stage and tore off the wigs of the two younger boys, throwing them down and grinding them under his heel. John watched, frozen with horror, as the Canon turned on Hugh.

'And you – you . . . you Jezebel, you harlot . . . you will rot in hell for ever . . .'

He grabbed Hugh's hair, pulling and tugging, tossing him this way and that across the platform like a rag doll. Hugh's hands went up to his head, pressing his fingers in hard, to soften the pain. Only when the Canon had wrenched out a bunch of his curls did he push Hugh to the ground. Hugh scrabbled away towards the Magister, who supported him down from the stage and lay him on the ground. The two younger boys cowered under the canopy at the back of the stage. Matthew stood aghast, pushing himself against the side of the dray. The Canon turned to face the silent crowd. With a crack, he brought down the scourge and held up the lock of Hugh's hair.

'Let there be an end to this blasphemy,' he said, his voice thundering out over the heads of the people. On and on he ranted till gradually, a few at a time, the crowd sank to its knees. Hugh lay huddled under the dray and John, dazed and angry, knelt beside him. Only the Magister remained standing, his eyes on Canon Senan as the tirade went on and on.

At last the torrent of fury began to ebb. His chest heaving, Canon Senan surveyed the abject crowd, still on their knees around the dray. He vaulted down and, beating the handle of the scourge in a staccato rhythm against his gown, he backed away. Crossing himself, he turned and went into the cathedral, under the outstretched arms of the Christ standing above the doors. Still in his hand was the lock of Hugh's hair.

For a long time, no one dared look up, but gradually, with hardly a word, the crowd began to melt away, just a few with their heads together whispering and glancing back at the cathedral doors. The Magister bent over Hugh and lifted him in his arms. With a curt movement of his head he indicated that the boys should follow him to the schoolhouse.

'Let's look at you, boy,' said the Magister when they were safely inside. He sat Hugh in his own big chair and looked at his head, gently parting the hair and smoothing it back. Hugh was white and shaking, a bald, red patch on his scalp beading with blood. The other boys huddled on the benches.

'How could he?' John burst out and thumped on the table. 'He had no right . . .'

'He had every right,' said the Magister, 'his was a righteous wrath. What he said was for the good of our souls. I should not have allowed . . .'

'But our play was for the good of souls, too,' said John. 'You said it was, and – and then you – we prayed . . .'

'Yes, yes,' said the Magister, 'but I reckoned without the crowd and . . .' He faltered and fell silent, his hand on Hugh's shoulder. Then after a moment he said, 'The Canon is . . . you must understand, the

Canon's zeal is for Christ. There are many who think that play-acting is wicked . . . he is only one of them but he speaks . . . speaks his mind. He uses powerful words, yes, but so that we are saved from torment. That is all.'

He sighed.

'The world turned upside down . . . I shall be glad when it is all over.'

'So will I . . . even more, now,' thought John, though about the Canon's zeal for his soul, he wasn't so sure.

'Sir,' said Fitz, 'will we – will we still go to the feast, to the Earl's feast tonight?'

The other boys looked up from tracing the patterns in the wood on the table with their fingers and looked more alert.

'Please, sir,' said Edward Longnose, 'we can, can't we?'

'Oh indeed,' said the Magister, 'we cannot possibly be so uncivil to the Earl as to stay away from his feast. But, Hugh, what about you? How do you feel?'

Hugh looked up at the Magister standing over him. 'Is it very bad?'

'Bad, my boy?'

'The hole in my hair.'

The Magister managed a smile. 'Nay,' he said, 'it's just a tiny patch. You have plenty left to cover it, isn't it so, John?'

John could see the blood still oozing, but he shook his head. 'You can hardly see it at all,' he said.

'They'll think you've taken your vows and have a tonsure,' said Edward Longnose with a grin.

Hugh's face fell and he put up a hand to his head again. 'Is it that big?'

John glared at Edward. 'Of course it's not that big. The rest of your hair will cover it up. Hugh, no one will notice. Honest.'

Hugh still looked anxious. 'Who else saw it happen? Did the other canons?'

'There were one or two at the back of the crowd, I believe,' said the Magister. 'Canon Humphrey was there . . .'

'And I saw Canon Gwyllim eating sweetmeats,' said Fitz, with feeling. 'But he stopped when . . .'

'But none of the others, I think,' said the Magister.

'Anyway,' said John, 'they'd be on your side. They don't like Canon Senan either . . . well, Canon Gwyllim doesn't.'

'John! Be quiet.'

The Magister looked up quickly and frowned.

'Now, Hugh, do you feel able to go to the feast or should you perhaps stay here in readiness for tomorrow? That's the most important thing, remember, the service and your sermon on Saint Nicholas' Day.'

'No, sir, please, I want to go. I can't miss the feast. The Earl can't have the feast without the Boy Bishop, can he? I'm feeling all right now, steadier . . . you know . . . it's only a bit of hair . . .' and he reached up his hand yet again, still a little doubtful.

'Good. Then off you go all of you. Wash your faces . . .'

'Twice in one day?'

The Magister affected not to hear Simon's whisper.

'Wash your faces and hands and tidy yourselves, then go back to the vestry. We will meet with the canons and the men choristers there and all of us walk to the Earl's manor together.'

'Well, what about all that?' said Peter Holt, as they went back to the dormitory. 'I wonder what made old Senan lose it like that?'

'He's always on the edge,' said Hugh. 'You know we've always said he's the one to really watch out for.'

'Yes, but . . .'

'D'you think he'll come to the feast?' said John.

'He'd better not,' said Fitz, raising his voice. 'Not after that . . .'

'Nobody's going to do anything about it if he does,' said Hugh. 'Don't tell me you lot are all going to face him out.'

Fitz gave a hurried shake of his head.

'And I'm not, that's for certain,' said Hugh, licking his finger and exploring the sore place among his curls. He looked at John. 'It feels quite big, big enough to stuff a pillow,' he said. 'Are you sure . . . ?'

'It probably feels big to you, but it hardly shows, does it?' said John, and the others gathered round making reassuring noises.

'Come on, then,' said Hugh. 'It's two miles through the woods to the Earl's manor and it's getting dark already.'

'Canon Gwyllim won't like all that walking,' said Edward Longnose. 'He's already been down the hill and back today.'

'He'll go if there's food at the end of it,' said Fitz.

'Quite right, too,' said Simon. 'I'm so hungry I'd walk to – to London for food if I had to.'

Cleanish and sort of tidy, they galloped over to the vestry where there was a rather low-key buzz of voices. News of Canon Senan's outburst had spread. Several of the men enquired about Hugh but he brushed their concern aside.

'Is he coming?'

John heard the Magister speak to Canon Humphrey. He must be asking if Canon Senan was coming to the feast.

'Nay.'

'He won't show his face.'

'Him? He's brass neck enough for anything. But if he doesn't approve of – of the play, then he won't approve of feasting to celebrate, will he?'

The Magister shook his head. 'I suppose not,' he said, 'though I mind he came last year, didn't he? But it wasn't all the plays, you know. Just ours . . . the one with Hugh as . . . as a girl . . . well, a . . .' He broke off, sensing that he might be overheard, and went off on a different tack. 'Will the Earl not be put out at his absence?'

'There's enough of us. I doubt he'll notice. We can always plead his illness.'

But with that, Canon Senan walked in. He looked round in the sudden silence. The boys held their breath. Had he come to forbid the feast?

'I cannot stop these – these celebrations,' he said, 'much though I would wish to do so.'

He appeared not to notice the quick, relieved smiles that darted round the room but leant forward on the table, drumming his fingers.

'We cannot be disrespectful to the Earl. But I admonish you to exercise restraint, my brothers in Christ. Remember. We are men of God and gluttony is a sin.'

He seemed to look straight at Canon Gwyllim as he spoke. The Canon dropped his head and shifted his weight about from foot to foot.

'I shall accompany you and wait outside the manor, praying for you all the while . . .'

'Great,' muttered Fitz.

'There will at least then be one of us sober enough to guide you all home safely if – if there has been overindulgence. But I beg you to remember . . . Tomorrow's . . . junketings . . . will be bad enough without having half of you sick from stuffing yourselves like Christmas geese.'

The look of disgust on his face was almost funny, but the boys thought better of laughing as he cracked his cane down on the table. One of the young canons went up to him. Canon Senan leant towards him as he spoke in his ear. His face seemed to soften a little and he nodded.

'Of course, my brother. If you feel it is against your conscience to attend this feast, you must stay here. Please pray for us.'

He blessed the young Canon and, with a glad smile, the young man turned back into the cathedral. Canon Senan seemed about to speak but changed his mind.

'Come then, if we must go, let us be away,' he said instead. He wheeled and set off towards the town field, his long strides forcing the boys almost to run to keep up with him. After a while, John began to struggle.

'I can't keep this up for two miles,' he said.

'Don't worry, he won't either. He just wants to make poor old Canon Gwyllim suffer a bit.'

'Why?'

Hugh shrugged. 'I told you, he likes to make anyone suffer. And Canon Gwyllim is easy meat.'

He flashed a quick grin and patted his stomach.

'Easy meat and plenty of it.'

John laughed. Hugh was feeling better.

The procession slowed down perforce when it came to the woods. The moon slid among the trees and the leader of each group lofted a lantern that cast long, flickering shadows on the narrow path before them. A wind sighed among the branches, shaking loose the last of the snow and powdering their faces as they passed under the black carapace of tangled boughs. In the distance a white owl hooted, caught in a moonbeam, as it wheeled and hovered over its prey on silent wings, and John spied a dog fox slipping away into the night like a sly, red spectre. Dead leaves rustled round their feet and brambles reached out from the undergrowth to drag at their clothes like sharp claws trying to pull them from the narrow path.

They trudged on huddled together in their small bands, their voices low and saying little. John thought of the return journey and shivered.

Chapter 11

Canon Senan led them to the manor. As they approached, there was a blast on a trumpet and the wicket gate to the stockade was flung open by a waiting soldier. The Canon entered and stood to one side. As the men and the boys passed him, he dropped to his knees, his eyes closed in fervent prayer.

The door of the manor opened wide and the Earl's steward greeted them with a low bow and a flourish. Behind him, it seemed to John that a myriad lamps and candles lit the great hall, sending out brilliant beams of light and warmth. With little more than a cursory glance at Canon Senan, the canons, the men, the boys all pressed forward, eager and excited at the sight of the food piled high on the long oak tables within. Between the arms of the tables running down from either end of the top table towards them, was a blazing fire, the smoke spiralling lazily up to a hole between the beams of the roof. High above, the length of one side of the hall, John's eye was caught by the glittering of glass in the tall, arched windows. The Earl stood by his chair at the centre of the top table, facing them.

'Where is my Bishop?' he called, holding his arms wide, a broad grin on his face. He was young and blue-eyed, not handsome but tall and strong and dressed in the finest of silks and satins, fur and leather, in crimson, yellow and a luminous jet black. His steward stood beside him, almost as resplendent in flamboyant colours that rivalled his master's. The Magister pushed Hugh forward.

'Here, my lord,' he said, 'here is Hugh, Lord Bishop for a day.'

'Come and sit beside me,' said the Earl.

Trying not to put up a hand to the sore place on his head, Hugh stepped forward shyly, past the long arm of the table, where a line of servants stood waiting, standing stiffly, the Earl's arms emblazoned on their chests. Hugh paused.

'Don't be shy,' said the Earl, still smiling. 'I won't eat you. Too much here for that,' and he swept an expansive arm towards the feast. Hugh still hesitated.

'Ah,' said the Earl, 'why not bring your own private chaplain with you? Would that help?'

Matthew glanced at the Magister, puffed out his chest and began to walk towards Hugh, but Hugh turned back towards the other boys.

'Peg,' he said and beckoned urgently, not noticing Matthew. 'Peg – er . . . John.'

'John, is it?' said the Earl, still smiling. 'That's it, bring your friend. He can be your private chaplain. That's fitting.'

Matthew looked thunder and dropped back, flushing red. The Magister glared round at the rest of the boys, daring them to laugh.

'Come on up, young fellow,' said the Earl, 'or we'll be here all night.'

The Magister gave John a shove towards Hugh and then stood beside Matthew, close to his shoulder, a restraining hand at the ready. John started what seemed a long journey to the top table, feeling every eye on his limp as he went. He reached Hugh and they went on together.

'Marked men,' thought John with a wry grin to himself, 'him with his bald patch and me with my devil's foot. All we need is a yellow badge.'

The Earl sat them down together and a servant brought a shiny gold cloak and a painted gold mitre. Ceremoniously, the Earl decked Hugh out in them, arranging the cloak over his high-backed chair. He looked round hastily for something for John, picked up a laurel wreath decorating the table and rammed it down over his ears, and everyone laughed and cheered.

'That's the best I can do,' he said.

John blushed and wrenched it up again, settling it on more comfortably. The cheers died down and he could hear Matthew's whinging voice even from up there.

'Be seated, everyone,' said the Earl. 'Let's have all the young lads up at this end. Men of the choir here and here' – he indicated the next level going down the two side tables – 'and the reverend canons below the salt. In order of precedence on this special occasion.'

He gave them an ironic bow.

Good-naturedly, the canons arranged themselves

at the bottom of the pecking order and everyone sat down, their feet among the rushes spread under the tables to catch droppings.

'Now who will bless our food for us all?' asked the Earl. 'Perhaps the Bishop's chaplain would oblige . . . ?'

John looked at him appalled. There was a kind of rumbling from one of the tables. Matthew. Under his breath he started a kind of a chant, 'The Bishop's chaplain . . . the Bishop's chaplain . . .'

One or two of the other boys, thinking it a great joke, joined in, banging on the table with their fists, 'Aye, aye . . . the Bishop's chaplain. The Bishop's chaplain . . .' and the chant was taken up round the tables. John gripped the arms of his chair in panic at the thought of speaking in front of all these people.

Suddenly, the Magister called out, topping the din. 'My lord, I think you will find the Bishop himself is prepared.'

'Excellent,' said the Earl, aware of John's desperation. He turned to Hugh. 'Well then, my lord?'

Hugh stood up, hampered by his cloak. The mitre slipped towards his nose and he straightened it impatiently, laughing all the while. He held up his hands for silence and in a strong, clear voice asked a blessing on the Earl, his family, his servants, his guests and, most of all, the food. John could hardly believe he was listening to Little Hugh, the butt of Matthew and the 'runt of the litter'. The Magister had done a good job. John looked down at him at the bottom of his table with a new respect.

'Let carousing commence. Serve the boys first!'

The Earl banged a tankard on the table and the feast began. In front of each guest was set a large square trencher of bread as a plate, a knife beside it. The doors opened and more servants brought in great platters of meat, goose, pork, venison, beef. Whole chickens and hams already lay on the table. Huge silver carp, their eyes bulging, their tails dangling over the edge of the dish, were followed by crayfish and lobster brought up from the coast that morning. Enormous jugs of beer and wine were emptied and refilled time and again. Simon's face was a study and the others hardly less so. The heat and the voices rose, and, like everyone else, John shovelled in food till he felt he would burst.

Giving himself a rest, John belched, sat back and watched the company. Down the table he could see the fat, pink hands of Canon Gwyllim, dropping chicken bone after chicken bone into the rushes, and another canon he did not know spearing a whole fish with his knife and ramming it into his mouth. Several men left the hall to relieve themselves outside, but as yet no one had disgraced themselves by throwing up at the table.

The Earl's steward was everywhere, supervising the serving of all the guests and especially Hugh and the Earl. For one fleeting moment he stood still, looking down the table, and a lamp sent his shadow on to the wall, catching John's attention. He frowned. Where had he seen that shadow before? The man himself he knew from seeing him in the cathedral and at the schoolhouse, but the shadow . . . He looked at Hugh, but Hugh was busy making the Earl laugh, not a difficult task, and one the Earl was clearly enjoying.

Turning back towards the tables, John found Matthew staring at Hugh with the eyes of – of a devil. He could think of no other word for it. Matthew suddenly sensed he was being watched and dropped his head, tearing a piece of meat to pieces with his hands as if he wished it were Hugh . . . or perhaps him, John. Probably either would do.

Suddenly, Hugh went pale, then a strange shade of green.

'Outside with you,' said the Earl, laughing and snatching off his mitre. Hugh threw off his cloak and dashed for the doors at the end of the hall, slipping and sliding in the now-greasy rushes.

John looked down at Matthew, who was laughing too, but not in the way the Earl was laughing. Matthew's eyes were cold as he watched Hugh's dash from the room. In his hand he clutched a ginger-bread man and he was plunging his knife into it till it fell to pieces on the table in front of him. Just to make sure, Matthew sliced off the head, threw it on the floor, half-stood and stamped on it just at the moment Hugh escaped through the door. Matthew must really believe he had the power to make Hugh ill by this stupid magic, first because he wasn't Boy Bishop, and now because Hugh hadn't chosen him to sit at the top table. At the sight of such hatred, John put his head in his hands. Feeling the laurel wreath, he took it off and tossed it between the empty dishes in front of him.

The Earl reached over and put a hand on his back. 'You too, oh Bishop's chaplain? Outside with you too?'

'Nay. Thank you, my lord, I'll do.'

John looked up and shook his head to clear it. He felt very tired. More wine was coming round and, from a gallery above him, musicians struck up a boisterous tune. Voices rose, John hardly believing the words the canons and the choir were bawling out. Simon, Edward Longnose and Fitz started to join in, bouncing around and pounding the table, but a glance from the Magister shut their mouths. The canons more than made up for it.

'Men of God, are they?' said the Earl, laughing. 'You wouldn't think so, to hear them.'

John craned his neck to look down the hall. Where was Hugh? He had been a long time.

'I think . . .' he said, standing up with difficulty, his head spinning.

'You too? I thought so,' said the Earl. 'Better run, eh?'

'No,' said John, 'it's just . . .'

But the Earl had turned to his steward and had lost interest.

As John passed Matthew, he kept a lookout, ready for a foot to trip him up or something to be 'accidentally' spilt on him. But all Matthew said was: 'Going to take care of our little boy? Good little Bishop's chaplain, then, are we?'

John took no notice but Matthew got up to follow him. Quickly, Edward Longnose upturned his almost full tankard of ale into Matthew's lap.

'Thanks, Edward,' muttered John, hurrying on and leaving the others to sort Matthew out – if they could. He reached the door to meet Hugh returning. He still looked pale, but gave John a watery smile.

'Lost it all,' he said ruefully, 'but it was worth it.'

The Magister stood up to meet them. 'It is time to go.'

'Oooh,' said Hugh, 'I was going to start all over again and the fun's just started. Listen.'

The discordant din of the singing grew wilder and more crude, the singers thumping the tables and stamping their feet, squelching about in the now squalid rushes. A couple of men choristers stood on the benches, prancing about lifting their gowns, showing their drooping hose. They attempted to link arms and circle round each other, whereupon they fell off into the filth, lying on their backs like landed fish, gasping for breath.

The Magister went up to the Earl. John and Hugh waited close to Canon Humphrey and Canon Gwyllim. The Earl's steward was pouring them yet more wine.

'You don't look so green now,' said John.

'I know. Pity we've got to go.'

'Did you see Canon Senan outside?'

'I forgot about him,' said Hugh. 'Funny, no, he wasn't there. I don't know where he was. Anyway, thank Saint Hugh he didn't see me. Imagine him if he saw the Boy Bishop chucking up into the bushes.'

The feast was drawing to a close. The Earl came down and shook Hugh's hand while the Magister and one or two of the other canons not quite the worse for wear started to gather up the loiterers.

'Hugh, go and tell Canon Senan we are on our way,' he said. Hugh looked at him in alarm, his hand flying up to his head.

'I was forgetting,' said the Magister. 'Where's Matthew? He can go.'

But Matthew was nowhere to be seen.

'Outside drying off, I expect,' said John. 'Don't worry, sir, I'll go.'

Hugh followed him outside. Most of the party were gathering inside the stockade fence. The soldier had gone and the gate was open to the path into the woods.

'Where is he?' said John.

'Have you seen Canon Senan?' Hugh asked around the waiting men.

'No, thank the good God,' said one. 'He's probably gone on ahead. Got tired of waiting.'

'Not him. If he said he'd wait, he'll wait,' said another. 'That'll be him,' and he nodded at a bobbing lantern a little way off through the trees. John started to limp towards it.

'Oh, what's the difference. It'll be quicker if I go. I won't be a minute,' said Hugh and he set off at a run.

'Wait for me,' called John, but Hugh had gone through the gate and vanished into the trees. The Magister and the rest of the boys emerged from the manor and the door closed behind them. Even with the lanterns, suddenly it seemed very dark. The men were jostling and changing groups. It was difficult to tell who was where but they finally sorted themselves out and straggled off towards the gate.

'Sir,' said John, uneasily, 'Hugh has gone on after Canon Senan. He's in the wood.'

'In the wood?' said the Magister. 'Why . . . ?'

John wanted to tug his arm, to hurry him along, but it took a few more minutes to organize a lantern for each group.

'Where's the light gone?' said John to Fitz.

'What light?'

'The light in the wood. Canon Senan – at least we thought it must be him . . . Hugh went to tell him we were on our way. But the light's gone out now.'

'He's probably on the way back,' said Edward Longnose. 'You can't always see the lanterns between the trees.'

John attached himself to the leading party, willing them to hurry, but they were mostly drunk, staggering and wandering off the path, pulling each other back, laughing and stopping to wet the bushes.

'Hugh!' John called. 'Hugh, where are you?'

The men were making too much noise for his voice to carry. He hurried on in the dark, feeling his way, limping and catching his feet in the roots of trees. The path twisted and turned, but he could still hear the voices behind him, cursing and swearing now the going was getting difficult. Suddenly, he stumbled. He put out a hand as he fell and touched damp flesh.

'One of the men, dead drunk,' he thought. He levered himself up, using the man's shoulder to press against. When he stood up, his hand was wet.

'Ugh!' he thought, 'vomit . . .' and he bent down to wipe his hand in the grass by the path as the first of the men carrying the lantern caught up with him.

'What's the matter?' said the man, slurring his speech.

He held up the lantern and John looked down at his hand. He drew in his breath sharply. His hand shone red in the lantern light. This wasn't vomit, it was blood. The man with the lantern tried to steady himself to look down at the man on the ground. He let out a terrible cry.

'Dear Christ!'

He backed away, crossing himself, and John grabbed the lantern as it was about to fall. He turned and looked down. Canon Senan lay on his back in a pool of blood. His arms were crossed on his chest. In one hand was his crucifix and in the other was the lock of Hugh's hair. His grey eyes were wide open as if he was looking up at the stars twinkling down through the bare branches. But Canon Senan would never see the stars again.

A night hawk clattered away suddenly, and a thin curtain of snow drifted down from the trees on to the Canon's cold face. John looked round into the darkness of the wood.

Hugh was nowhere to be seen.

Chapter 12

'Why can't I be Boy Bishop now? I know the service. I can do it. You know I can.'

'Matthew,' said the Magister for the third or fourth time, as calmly as he could, 'one of our brothers in Christ is dead . . . brutally murdered . . . can you not see . . . ?'

'But—'

'And Hugh is missing. We shall have to join the search for him as soon as it is light. Matthew, can you not understand that the world is already upside down enough without making it more so? This is not the time for – for celebrations.'

At last Matthew saw that the Magister meant what he said. He looked round angrily at the other boys, huddled on their pallet beds in the dormitory, pale and upset.

'I should have been Boy Bishop,' he said, spitting out his words, 'then none of this would have happened. Hugh . . .' His voice trailed off in disgust.

'What about Hugh?' said Edward Longnose. 'Where is he?'

The Magister shook his head. 'I don't know,' he said. 'Perhaps he came back with a later group.'

'Then why isn't he here? They must all be back by now. Why aren't we out looking for him?' said John. 'He's out there somewhere, maybe hurt, maybe dead.'

'Not him,' said Matthew, with a snide, one-sided grin. 'Didn't you see? Didn't any of you notice?'

'See what?' said Fitz, getting up and coming over to him.

'What was in Canon Senan's hand.' Matthew held up his clenched fist, shook it slightly, and thrust it towards each boy in turn.

'No,' said Simon, 'what?' and he got up too.

John stayed very quiet. He had seen the lock of hair the Canon held but had said nothing. He looked at Matthew, a knot of fear clutching his stomach. He knew what was coming.

'It was Hugh that killed the Canon.'

'Matthew, what are you saying?' said the Magister.

'It was his hair that was in his hand. I saw it. Hugh killed him to get his revenge for what the Canon did at the play . . .'

The boys looked at each other stunned. John sent the Magister a mute appeal, but the Magister said nothing. He stood looking thoughtful, a small frown creasing his forehead.'

'Hugh wouldn't do that,' said John, blurting out his words. 'You know he wouldn't, Matthew . . . all of you . . . don't you . . . don't you . . .'

He knew there would be no answer. Only Edward Longnose looked at him directly. The others turned away or dropped their eyes.

'I didn't know it was Hugh's hair that he had . . .'

said Edward. 'Peg, it sounds as if . . .'

'No,' shouted John.

The Magister sighed. 'John, it looks suspicious.'

John rounded on him. 'Tell me, how do you think Hugh could have killed him? He's not big enough, not strong enough . . .'

The Magister backed away. 'John, have a care. You forget yourself.'

'I – I'm sorry, sir,' said John, then cautiously, 'Sir. How – how did the Canon die?'

'His head was beaten in with a heavy branch. It was lying close beside him,' said the Magister. He put up a hand to his mouth and he closed his eyes in distress as he thought of the body lying on the ground, the blood like a deep, shining red halo round its head. Most of the boys he had kept back so they did not see, but he had seen enough himself.

'Well,' said John, with a glare at Matthew. 'Sir, can you really imagine "Little Hugh" beating the Canon to death? He couldn't have reached for one thing. Canon Senan is – was – tall.'

'Perhaps he was praying,' said Matthew quickly, 'kneeling down . . .'

'In the woods?' said Edward Longnose.

'Anywhere,' said Matthew. 'You know what he was like.'

'He was at the door of the manor when he started his prayers,' said the Magister. 'I do not think he would have gone into the woods to finish them. There would have been no reason. He must have gone with someone.'

'Hugh,' said Matthew, 'to make his confession for

dressing up as a girl. That's what upset the Canon. Trust the little runt Hugh. Asking forgiveness! Huh! Sickening. But clever, clever . . .'

The boys still looked uneasy, their thoughts wrenched this way and that, not knowing what to believe.

'Whether he killed the Canon or no,' said the Magister, 'he will have to be found.'

'We should be looking now,' said John, clenching his fists. 'We shouldn't be leaving him . . . out there . . .'

'We could see nothing if we went in the dark,' said the Magister. 'There would be more of us lost. We will go as soon as we can see. If Hugh did kill the Canon he will have to face the consequences; if he did not . . .'

'If he didn't,' said John, his heart sinking, 'he has run because he knows who did do it and is afraid, or – or someone has taken him away. He may even be . . .'

John started to shake almost uncontrollably. There must be no more death . . . no more death . . .

Fitz came and put a hand on his shoulder, and he slumped down on to the pallet bed. The Magister lifted his legs, laying him down, shivering and stiff.

'Peace, John. We can do nothing now. All of you,' said the Magister. 'Try and sleep. We must be out early to look for Hugh. I will stay with you.'

Without bothering to take off their gowns, the boys lay on their little beds, huddled together, worried and afraid. The Magister went downstairs to see that the door was closed.

'There must be something in it, if he is to stay with us all night,' said Simon in a whisper.

'If Hugh's dead . . .' said Edward Longnose. 'But why should he be dead?'

'We'll be next . . .' and with a little cry, one of the younger boys put the blanket up to his ears and lay sucking his thumb, his eyes big in the dark.

The Magister returned and they dozed fitfully, the sound of his quiet prayers calming them a little. But John lay next to Fitz, rigid, unable to toss and turn in case he should disturb him. Nor did he want the Magister to see he was awake, his mind racing, the Magister's muttered prayers only interrupting his thoughts and keeping sleep away.

Canon Senan's body had lain in the wood all night, with two of the braver canons kneeling at his side in the pale beam of a lantern, their chins resting on chilled, folded hands. At first light, others had returned with a pallet to lift him over the rough path, too difficult to negotiate with such a load in the dark. The boys passed the sad little cortège on its way to the infirmary, where the Canon was laid in the small chapel, prayers for his soul rising to heaven like the smoke of the candles burning around him, till he should be wound into his shroud and taken to the cathedral. Someone had removed the lock of hair from his hand.

Hugh had not returned. There was no sign of him in the schoolhouse, the vestry nor in the cathedral itself. The Magister and the boys gathered at the entrance to the wood, many of them bleary, their heads throbbing in the glare of the frosty morning.

'Please, sir, let's keep together,' said Simon, looking into the trees and hanging back.

'There will be more chance of finding him if we divide into two groups at least,' said the Magister. 'I will take this path directly back towards where we found the – where we found Canon Senan. Towards the manor. Perhaps he went back there.'

He looked at Matthew.

'Will you take the other party, Matthew?'

'Sir,' said Matthew, 'please, sir, I don't feel . . . I'm sick. I don't think I . . .'

With a look almost of relief the Magister said hurriedly, 'Go back to the dormitory, Matthew. Sit quietly till we return. It is useless taking someone who will be a liability. Edward, you, John, Fitz and Simon go that way. I'll take Peter Holt and the younger ones.'

Matthew, his shoulders bowed and indeed looking peaky, slouched off back towards the dormitory. The Magister took the main path, spreading his boys out a little way on either side. They disappeared into the trees, lifting their legs high over the brambles, calling Hugh's name as they went.

Edward Longnose pointed to a side path leading off into the denser part of the wood. 'That way?' he said.

The path seemed to twist and turn, getting narrower as it went and the trees closer together. The odd shaft of winter sun darted between the branches, but the rest of the wood was dark and forbidding.

'Wait,' said John. He looked round at the three

lads standing together, looking down the path, clearly not relishing the depths of the wood, even with all of them together. 'Do you – do you believe he – that Hugh could have done it?'

Fitz shrugged. 'Someone did,' he said, 'and we don't know where they are, Hugh or whoever it was. Suppose they're down there – waiting for us . . .' He nodded towards the wood.

'Well, it wasn't Hugh,' said John, with a firm nod of his head on each word.

Last night, wide awake, he had wondered how Matthew had known about the lock of hair in Canon Senan's hand. Matthew hadn't been there when John found him, and the Magister had got everyone away quickly before they could see. And where had he gone earlier? But there was enough suspicion and fear without arousing more. They must find Hugh and sort everything out later.

Fitz shrugged again. 'Let's go if we've got to,' he said and the others fell in behind him. John brought up the rear. At first they were quiet, then John started to shout Hugh's name.

'Hush!' said Simon.

'What do you mean, hush?' said John. 'If we don't shout we might miss him . . . he might miss us . . . the Magister's lot were shouting . . .'

'It just seems . . .' Simon gazed round into the silent trees. A sudden wind sighed through the branches, making them creak; a twig cracked and all was still.

Fitz shivered. 'I know what you mean. It just seems as if we might . . . well, wake . . . wake . . .'

'The dead,' said Simon, panic in his eyes, and he

turned and raced back the way they had come.

'Don't let him go . . .' said John.

'I don't blame him,' said Fitz. 'It's not . . . There's something creepy . . . I . . .'

'I don't like it either,' said Edward Longnose, 'but we've got to find Hugh. So come on. But, Peg, just don't shout too loud. It makes echoes and . . .'

'All right,' said John, and they set off again in silence, beating at the bushes with sticks they foraged from the undergrowth. After a while, the narrow path divided. One way led to a clearing and a promise of fewer trees and more light. The other led deeper into the wood.

'This way,' said Edward, choosing the clearing without stopping to think.

'You go that way,' said John. 'I'm going this way.'

'You can't go on your own,' said Edward, 'not down there.'

'No,' said Fitz, 'the Magister would say to keep together. I know he would.'

'But he didn't say it, did he?' said John. 'And the wider we spread the more likely we are to find him.'

'What if you fall?' said Edward, looking at John's foot.

'Then I get up again,' said John and he swung away from them down the second path before they could stop him. They called him once or twice without much enthusiasm, then gave up and went their own way.

For a while he could hear them, thrashing away at the bushes, one of them occasionally calling Hugh's name in a small voice that seemed to quaver away into nothing. He was glad to be on his own. He called loudly as he went, using his stick to steady him on the rough trail, avoiding the gnarled roots that crossed it here and there. Occasionally he struck out, beating his way into the undergrowth when he saw something that just might have been a blue gown, a mop of fair hair, a pale face, but it never was, and he returned to the path.

Suddenly, ahead of him, more light seemed to trickle down through the trees and he thought he could see grey stone, a wall, a building maybe, between them. He hurried on.

The wood opened out and in the centre of a patch of grass, bright with frost in the weak winter sun, stood a square building, small in girth and not quite a tower but tall, with a small, barred window, far too high to reach. John approached as quietly as he could. The door was heavy, with an iron lock, and studded with massive nails. He circled the building, looking for other ways in, but there was nothing, only the door and the high window. He took the door handle in both hands and tried to ease it open. He shook the handle and pushed at the door, but the lock was firm. There was no way he could get it open and there was only one way to find out if Hugh, or anyone else, was inside. He took a deep breath and yelled.

'Hugh! Hugh! Are you in there?'

He laid his ear to the door. At first he heard nothing, but then he thought he heard movement.

'Hugh!' he called again.

This time, he was certain he heard a faint cry.

Someone was locked in there and it might be Hugh. Another shout brought nothing. He must get inside somehow.

Looking round, he saw a tree with a single branch stretching towards the high window. He managed to clamber up, losing his clogs on the way, then sat astride and started to inch himself along. The branch dipped alarmingly and he waited for it to steady itself. He craned forward and found he could just see in to a corner of the room below. On the earth floor inside lay a dark shape. He called again.

Whoever it was stirred and he saw a hand, quite a small hand, move into a patch of light, as if the owner was trying to crawl forward towards it.

'Hugh! Is that you? It's Peg . . .'

A second hand joined the other as if trying to push the person up from the ground. They collapsed, and John saw Hugh's yellow curls land on top of them, almost covering them. His head rolled to one side, leaving the hands, palm upwards, the fingers curled. His eyes were closed.

He'd found him. John had found him. But what to do now? At first he wondered if he could cross to the window and squeeze through the bars. But it was too high to jump down inside – it would be the end of his foot. And anyway, if he did get in, the door was locked and he couldn't get out. There was no point in both of them being prisoners.

He slithered down as best he could and hammered on the door. He didn't think there was anyone else inside, but he didn't care if there was, nor if anyone could hear him out here in the wood. There was no sound from Hugh, but he had been alive, he had . . . He must get help.

Without stopping to pick up his clogs, he half-ran, half-staggered back through the wood, branches whipping at his face, slipping on the frosted pathway. He stumbled to the schoolhouse and then the dormitory. Empty. Where was the Magister? Why wasn't he here? Didn't he care about Hugh? Of course, of course, everyone was still searching the wood.

He hesitated, panic rising in his chest. Who should he go to? The canons . . . but he suddenly realized that any of them might have killed Canon Senan . . . they had all been in and out of the feast during the evening. Any one of them could have done it. How could he trust them?

Who else? He looked round. It was still early. The few men in the marketplace wouldn't understand what he was talking about and they would fetch the canons anyway. Why didn't the Magister come?

Suddenly, striding towards him, came Reuben ben Ezra. John hesitated, squared his shoulders, then bolted across the square towards him.

'Sir,' he said, 'I need help.'

The Jew put his hands out and grasped John's shoulders to stop him.

'Sir, is it?' said Reuben ben Ezra with a smile. 'Help from me, young gentile?'

'Please,' said John, 'it's my friend. He's locked up. In the wood. There's a stone building . . . Please . . . I couldn't get to him. I think he's hurt.'

'How did he come to be there?' asked Reuben, his smile fading.

'I don't know. It's because of Canon Senan . . .'

'He put him there?'

'No, no. Please come, I can't explain now. Canon Senan's dead . . .'

Reuben ben Ezra muttered something in Hebrew.

'Please just come.'

John tugged at the arm with its yellow badge, willing him to follow him into the trees. But Reuben stopped.

'John – yes, I know your name from my son – I cannot come with you like that. It might be said I was . . . If I pass the time of day with you that is one thing, but going with you into the wood on this errand in view of the world would be . . .'

He tried to prise John's fingers from his arm. A sudden shout made them look up.

'Here,' he said, 'here is the Magister. He is the man you need. Now let me go,' and he turned and strode away.

The Magister hurried over. John turned to face him.

'What were you doing with Reuben ben Ezra, boy?' he said, angrily.

'I've found Hugh,' said John. 'I couldn't find you. I need help to get him out . . . I was asking . . .'

'Help from a Jew? What are you thinking of?'

'Of Hugh . . . sir. I had to ask someone and you weren't here. I tell you, I've found him.'

The Magister flushed. 'Even so. Where is he?'

'In a sort of cell in the wood. He couldn't answer

me, I think he's hurt. But I saw him, I saw him, sir. Please come . . .'

Angrily, he started to tug at the Magister, who pushed him away.

'John, pull yourself together. You saw Hugh in a building in the wood?'

'Yes, he's locked in. Oh please . . . please . . .'

'I see. Wait there.'

He called the younger boys, who were straggling along behind him, looking tired and dispirited.

'Peter Holt,' he said, 'take them to the schoolroom and – and just, oh, keep them occupied somehow. I will be back as soon as I can.'

Peter nodded and started to prod and poke the younger boys towards the schoolhouse. Fitz and Simon stuck their heads out of the door and hollered a greeting. So they hadn't wasted much time hunting for Hugh.

'Now,' said the Magister. 'Tell me properly.'

Why could the man not understand the urgency . . . ? Fists clenched, John forced himself to explain as calmly as he could how he had found Hugh and come back for help, how he had found the schoolhouse empty and how Reuben ben Ezra happened to be there.

'You must never, never do that again, John,' said the Magister.

'No, sir, no,' said John, clenching his fists, trying to keep calm.

'I am a patient man' – John glanced up at him – 'and I know you are upset, but there are things that you must not do, and to go to the Jew, any of the

Jews, for help, is one of them. Do you understand?'

'Yes . . . sir,' said John, taking a deep breath, 'but please, please come now.'

The Magister nodded. With a glance back at Peter Holt shepherding the last of the boys into the schoolhouse, he followed John's limping run towards the trees.

'Slowly, boy,' he said. 'More haste, less speed.' But John hurried on, turning impatiently now and again for the Magister to catch up. Breathless and getting more irritable by the minute, the Magister insisted on a moment's rest, forbidding John to go on ahead or they would both get lost. They passed the place where the path divided and at last John saw the grey stone among the trees ahead of them. He raced forward, almost falling flat as his foot gave way beneath him. The Magister grabbed him and supported him as he hobbled into the clearing.

'Here?' said the Magister.

John nodded. But as he nodded his heart lurched. The heavy door was open and inside, the stone building was empty.

'He was here,' he said. 'I know he was. I saw him.'

'How did you see him?' said the Magister. 'If the door was locked. How could you see in?'

'I called and I thought I heard someone inside, sort of . . . trying to answer,' said John, swallowing hard at the memory, 'and I – I climbed up there to look through the window.'

The Magister looked up at the branch of the tree and closed his eyes for a moment.

'John, John,' he said, shaking his head, 'you could have killed yourself.'

'But I didn't,' said John, angrily, going into the stone cell. 'I needed to see who was there. If it was Hugh . . . and it was . . . sir, I know it was. I saw his hair. A bit of his face. He was in that corner. He tried to get up when I called but he couldn't . . . he . . .'

Exhausted, his knees gave way. He slithered his back down the stone wall, put his head on his knees and cried.

The Magister hesitated then knelt beside him. 'All right, John. All right. Stop now.' He put a hand on his shoulder. 'John, I believe you. At least, I believe you saw someone or something. An animal, a sheep perhaps, hurt and kept in here for the night. Perhaps it was a sheep's curls you saw . . . But from up there . . .' He glanced over his shoulder at the tree outside. 'You wanted it to be Hugh . . .'

John looked up. He wiped his eyes on his sleeve, sniffed hard and scrambled to his feet. 'No,' he said, his voice low and tense, 'I saw him . . . sir,' and he hit the side of his fist against the wall, hard.

The Magister sighed angrily. 'You cannot be sure what you saw, John. There is no sign of him here now. I have no reason to believe he was ever here. You saw what you wanted to see. Now . . .' He let out a deep breath. 'Now, let us return and decide what to do next. He may – he may even have returned while we are wasting our time.'

True, Hugh just might have come back. John flung himself past the Magister, allowing himself a glimmer of hope. Outside the building, he spied his clogs under the tree. He shoved his feet in them and set off down the path, dot-and-carry, the Magister panting along behind him. He threw open the schoolhouse door. There was bedlam inside, the younger boys playing tig over the benches and the older boys yelling encouragement.

'Is he here?' said John, catching his breath.

'Who?' said Edward Longnose.

'Hugh, of course. Has he come back?'

'Shut up a minute,' yelled Edward, quelling the riot. He saw the Magister coming across the square. 'The Magister's coming.'

The boys rushed to their seats and pretended to be working. Edward shook his head.

'He's not here,' said John, wheeling round on the Magister as he came in. 'I just thought – hoped you might be right but . . .'

He sat at the table with his head in his hands.

'He was out there. I know it was him. I saw his face. Someone's got him. Someone's taken him away.'

He looked up at the Magister, breathing quickly, his hands gripping the table. Once he had respected this man, thought him strong, thought him to be trusted.

'You know I'm right. Someone's taken him.'

The Magister turned away.

Chapter 13

John searched the cathedral, first the nave, then round into the apse, Saint Aelred's shrine, the vestry. He peered into the choir. When it was empty, he looked in the dormitory, upstairs and down, and in the bushes round the square. He went into the blacksmith's forge; he spoke to the tailor. He badgered everyone he could see. But no one had seen Hugh.

He put his head into Canon Humphrey's kitchen, but Rufus made a business of pressing his lips together for John to hush as the cook banged pots about him in a furious temper. John grabbed a crust and a cheese rind and left.

Outside the west door the crowd was gathering, excited, agog, ready for the next of the revels.

'Silence! Pray silence! Listen . . .'

John pushed through the crowd to see what was happening as Canon Gwyllim stepped out of the west door, looking nervous, holding up his hands, his voice hardly audible. The noise from the crowd began to subside into an expectant hush as they scented a drama.

'People of . . . er . . . my er . . . brothers and sisters in Christ . . .'

'Go on! Spit it out!' yelled a voice, to be instantly silenced.

'I regret that there has been an – an accident . . . Our – our beloved' – Canon Gwyllim swallowed the lie – 'our *beloved* Canon Senan whom you all know well, is – is dead.'

The crowd gasped.

'God called him . . . it was very sudden . . . very sudden . . . last night. It has been . . . shocking and – and shocking . . .' He crossed himself. 'Masses will be said . . . We feel . . . we feel it is not fitting that today's ceremony should take place . . .'

His voice faltered.

'I am sure you will understand . . .' he said, his voice breaking as he turned away, went in through the door and closed it behind him. Listening from the back of the crowd, John could picture the Canon leaning against the door inside, his hands shaking. Uncertain what to make of this news, the crowd slowly scattered, murmuring, muttering, mostly puzzled, shocked or even frightened, some cursing in disappointment, and here and there, one or two perhaps sad, but rumour and conjecture already spreading.

'He was terrible in his rage,' said one old man, 'but he never deserved to go so quick like that . . .'

'Wonder what it was took him?' said another.

'Aye. I wonder. That temper of his . . .' said the first, with a knowing look.

'He was taken by the will of God,' said a stern-looking man in rich clothes, looking down disdainfully.

'It comes to us all,' said the old man, glaring back at him. The rich man walked away quickly towards the vestry door, jingling the purse at his belt. Canon Humphrey came out and spoke to him briefly as a sudden clatter of hooves rang out across the cobbles. The Earl's steward jumped down from his horse, handing the reins to a page who had been riding behind him. As he turned to Canon Humphrey, the winter sun, suddenly brilliant, cast a brief shadow on the vestry door.

Suddenly, John remembered ... it was the Earl's steward who had been upstairs at Canon Humphrey's that night, and had left with Canon Gwillym long after the curfew. The steward hurried into the vestry and Canon Humphrey, with an apologetic nod to the rich man, turned and followed him in. John heard the words 'Canon Senan' and 'tragedy' before the door closed. Hypocrites. They had all hated him, or were afraid of him, he was sure. But they must all know that Hugh was missing too and no one was doing anything about it. Why wasn't everyone turning the place upside down to find him? The Magister seemed to have given up and the canons never even started. They didn't care ... none of them ...

He sat down on the stones of the vestry porch, his head aching. He must do something. Did he dare ask the Earl's steward if he knew anything? The murmur of voices inside grew louder and he drew back out of the way. The door was flung open.

'I'll come back tomorrow ...'

The Earl's steward passed him and was gone

without a glance. He swung himself up on his horse, his page behind him, and trotted away towards the wood. From inside the vestry, John heard Canon Humphrey say:

'He's right. There is no place for them in this city. Jews . . . They are nothing but trouble.'

'Can you believe it? They sacrifice . . . They sacrifice children . . . you have heard? Children . . . in their heathen rituals . . .' Canon Gwyllim's voice grew louder and more hysterical as he drew near the door.

John stood up quickly and flattened himself against the wall.

'Hush,' said Canon Humphrey. 'Let's hear no more about children from you.'

As the Canon leant out to close the door, John vanished round the corner, just in time, but there was a footfall behind him.

'Gotcha, ye little bleeder.'

Before he could move, the pedlar grabbed him by the arm and swung him round to face him, his mean little face pushed close to John's.

'What ye doin' there? Listenin', were ye?'

'No,' said John. 'And anyway, what's it to you? Let me go.'

He pulled his arm free but the pedlar barred his path.

'Got a long nose, have we? Like to know what's goin' on?'

He reached a hand towards John's face as if to twist his nose. With his own forearm, John smashed his arm away so hard the man winced. For a moment he looked as if he might strike back, but thinking better of it, he gave a weaselly grin, showing his yellow fangs, and poked a finger at John's chest.

'Can't take a joke, eh?'

'You don't joke,' said John, glancing down at the hand an inch away from him. He stared. The hand was red, red with blood, surely. He looked up slowly.

'That's blood . . .'

'So?'

'Did you . . . Was it . . . ?'

He backed away, then turned. Behind him, he heard the pedlar hawk and spit, then cackle with laughter as he bawled out, 'Devil got in yer foot, Twister?'

John hurried away to the edge of the square. He needed to think. He felt as if his head were being battered from inside. Was it the pedlar who had killed Canon Senan? He had reason to hate him, marching him out of the cathedral that time for everyone to see. And now John was certain he had blood on his hands . . . but then, he killed animals. Hugh had said so.

He looked down over the edge of the escarpment. Way below him, Aaron was coming out of his house. He watched him stand still for a moment, then go round to the little garden at the back, tucked into the cliffside out of sight.

Sacrifices. John could clear up one of the questions in his head, here and now. He must talk to Aaron.

John looked at the rocks over which the waterfall tumbled straight down into a pool in the garden. Could he manage to climb down? That way no one would see him go in through the gate; they wouldn't know where he was going. He tucked his gown into his belt and swung himself down over the edge of the cliff, keeping to the side of the stream, where splinters of ice shimmered in the foam. Once he could have done this with ease, but now . . .

He climbed down steadily, keeping his weight on his good foot as best he could, feeling for footholds with the injured one, changing over quickly by hanging from his fingers. Under his hands, just for a moment, the stones felt familiar and safe, as if they belonged there, and he thought of the last angel, high up in the cathedral. Sometimes an eddy of freezing water splashed his face, making him splutter. Suddenly he missed his footing and sent a pebble bouncing and rattling down the cliff.

'Peg! What are you doing? Come down. You mustn't . . .' Aaron was looking up at him in alarm, his hands together, shoulders round his ears, his Jew's hat shading his eyes. 'Please, come down . . .'

'It's – quite – safe,' said John, breathing fast.

'No, no, it isn't that . . .'

John stumbled down the last few feet and toppled as he landed at the bottom by the pool, his hand in the clear water.

'Take your hand away,' said Aaron urgently.

'It's all right, I'm not very wet,' said John, taking it out and shaking it, the drops rippling the surface.

'You don't understand. That is the mikveh, our sacred water. It must be kept *pure*.'

'Oh!'

John snatched his hand away and dried it quickly on his woollen hose.

'I'm sorry . . . I didn't mean . . . I didn't know . . .'

'No. Of course. But we live here because of the stream. It is straight from the side of the hill, you see, and nothing touches it till it comes into the pool. So we use it for . . . for . . .'

John took a breath. 'Rituals?' he said.

'Yes,' said Aaron, smiling, 'rituals of all kinds. Many rituals. I don't even know them all yet.'

Aaron sat beside him. The water John had spilled was already freezing on the tiles by the pool. John lowered his head and concentrated on rolling a pebble back and forth. Aaron looked at him, his smile fading.

'What is wrong?'

'I don't know how to . . .'

'Peg, tell me.'

John looked up. 'I have to ask you . . .'

'Yes?'

'I – I can't.'

'Yes, you can. Ask me what? Peg, what is this terrible thing you have to ask me that you can't – ask me?'

'If I ask you, you won't speak to me any more. I wouldn't if it were me.'

Aaron laughed. 'If I were you I would just ask it, then we'll see.'

'I have heard . . . I heard one of the canons . . . he said . . .'

'The canons, other people, say many things about us.'

154

John looked at him. 'Aaron, do you sacrifice children?'

Aaron drew back. 'Do I what?'

'He said that Jews . . .' John swallowed. 'He said that Jews sacrificed children in their rituals, and—'

Aaron gasped. 'No. No, we don't. No!' He shook his head again and again, his fingers twisting in his lap.

'I told you you'd be angry,' said John. 'But I had to ask.'

'Certainly you did,' said Reuben ben Ezra, behind him, 'but better you had asked me, perhaps, young gentile. Now what is this about?'

Reuben settled on a boulder by the pool. Gradually, the story of the murder of Canon Senan, Hugh's disappearance, the blood on the pedlar's hands, and Canon Gwyllim's crying out about Jewish rituals, came spilling out.

'So it seems that there are many people who might have done this – this evil thing. Well, whatever the truth, this will bode ill for us,' said Reuben, with a sigh, rising up and towering over John. 'And I can tell you now, John, that it is better that you leave here quickly and do not come here again.'

'But . . .'

'You must not be seen speaking to us. It is for your sake, not ours.'

'Why? You are the only ones who listen to me.'

Reuben sighed. 'Nevertheless, it is dangerous. Believe me, they do not listen to us either. John, we cannot help you. We dare not. You are not safe here.'

'I don't understand. I don't understand anything.'

John dropped his head, tears building behind his closed eyes. Reuben put out a hand and rested it on his shoulder and John did not try to pull away.

'The times are troubled,' said Reuben. 'For us, for you, for everyone it seems. Perhaps one day . . . But now you must go. Come with me.'

Still holding his shoulder, he led John to the stone wall at the end of the tiny garden.

'There is a pathway that leads back along the side of the hill and then up to the town field,' he said. 'Provided no one sees you climb over the wall, they will not worry too much about where you have been if you go that way. Do *not* go the other way towards the houses of my brethren. And John . . .'

Very gently he turned John to face him. Beside him, Aaron stood in silence, his hands folded.

'We do not sacrifice children. We do not drink blood. We did not kill your Christ,' said Reuben.

John nodded. 'I know,' he said. 'I believe you. So why are you marked then?' He glanced angrily at Reuben's yellow badge.

'Hush. For the same reason that you are said by some people to be marked too. Hmm? Ignorance and fear, young Christian. Ignorance and fear.'

He patted John's shoulders once, twice, then, 'Off with you,' he said and between them Reuben and Aaron heaved him over the high wall and listened for him to drop safely the other side. With little more than a grunt, he scrambled up.

'Shalom, Peg,' called Aaron, his soft voice hardly audible from inside the garden.

'God go with you,' said Reuben.

'And with you,' said John.

With a glance in each direction to make sure he hadn't been seen, he set off along the path, his gown swishing through the frosty grass. The shadow of the cathedral loomed over him and on down the side of the hill, cold and forbidding. After a while he paused. He felt as if someone was watching him. He looked up but the skyline of the hill above was deserted, only the silhouette of the towers of the cathedral jutting up into the sky beyond it. On he went, leaving the path and gradually climbing the hill as he went.

Again the uneasy feeling stopped him and as he looked up and behind him, a figure whisked away out of sight.

Matthew. How long had he been following? How much had he seen? John was so sure he had been careful, but ... He climbed the hill and started to cross the square towards the schoolhouse when a terrible scream tore out, bouncing off the cathedral walls, echoing down into the valley, reaching the city and reverberating from the towers of the churches below. Everyone in the square seemed to freeze. After a moment, they turned towards the well standing close to the top of the pathway down into the city.

A woman was standing there. Her rough sacking apron was over her head, her hands to her face, her wooden bucket on its side spinning round on its side at her feet, dribbling water. She shrieked and shrieked until a man caught hold of her and shook her, tearing back the apron from her face.

'What is it? What?'

She pointed into the well, her hand shaking, her head turned away.

'The water . . . turned to blood . . .' she said.

The gathering crowd drew back. They looked at the bucket spinning slower and slower. It was empty and the little water spilt there might have been any colour on the grey cobbles.

'A miracle,' came a whisper.

'Nah,' said the man who held the woman. He strode forward and peered into the well.

'That's no miracle. There's something . . . someone down there.'

'Dear God . . .'

'Sweet Jesu . . .'

'Holy Mother . . .'

The crowd began to cross themselves, to run, to hold on to one another, to drop on to their knees, wailing, beating their breasts. Three or four of the men started to collect rope and a ladder, shouting and clearing the way, preparing to pull up whoever it was. The well was not deep. It would not take long. John stood very still. With a heart like lead, he closed his eyes. He knew who it would be.

Chapter 14

They laid Hugh in a side chapel almost beneath the last angel. The procession passed close to Canon Senan in his white shroud, lying in a side chapel, his chin bound up in white cloth to keep his thin mouth closed for ever.

'Not near him,' John burst out. The Magister looked at him fiercely but said nothing, and they moved on.

Hugh too was all in white, his yellow curls peeping out from the linen binding, the sore patch covered. Like the Canon, his arms were crossed on his chest but his hands were bare, for all the world to see. On his palms were two bloody marks, the marks of the stigmata, the marks of Christ crucified.

Some were saying it was a miracle. Others were saying different.

Peter Holt and Simon, Fitz and Edward Longnose laid the bier down with scarcely a wobble. John had wanted to help carry it, but the Magister had said no and now John could understand why. Too precarious if he had carried it. Not only his foot was unsteady. He had not stopped shaking since they took Hugh's body from the well.

The canons came and started to light candles to begin the mass. For hours, across the nave, others had been saying mass for Canon Senan. The prayers went on and on. John looked up at the angels drifting across the distant ceiling, glittering and remote, and looked away.

Outside the cathedral the mob were baying for blood.

'Down with the Jews! Killers, murderers!'

'Out with them . . . 'ang them up!'

'Drinkers of blood . . . sacrifices . . . our children . . .'

John glanced at the Magister's set face.

'Sir . . .' said John, touching his sleeve.

But the Magister snatched his arm away. 'No, John. They are right. They should not kill the Jews, not in that way, but what they are saying is right. This is a blood sacrifice. And who else would do that? They have crucified . . . crucified, do you understand . . . ? They crucified Hugh as they once crucified . . .' and he bowed his head.

'I don't believe it, sir.'

'You have the evidence of your own eyes.' The Magister made a brief gesture towards Hugh's folded hands with the marks of the nails in the upturned palms.

'They didn't . . . they wouldn't . . .' John's voice was firm.

'What do you know of what they would or would not do? And who else would it be?'

John said nothing. He didn't know who else it would be, not yet, but he would, and the Magister had made up his mind about it without thinking, like all those people yelling outside. John was certain it wasn't Reuben or any of the Jews. Someone else had done it, killed Hugh, killed Canon Senan. Or maybe two different people. But who else *would* have done these terrible things? And why? His mind raced round and round – the feast, Canon Senan, the lock of hair, the building in the wood. Who . . . who?

'Yes, tell us who, Peg-leg. Just who do you think would have done it?'

Still John said nothing as Matthew, kneeling in front of him, turned round to hiss over his shoulder.

'Can't say? Won't say? You know very well who it is. You know it's the Jews . . . all of them. I've seen you with them, Peg-leg, and I know. Are you sure you didn't have something to do with it yourself? That's it! You've been softening Hugh up all the time, pretending to be his friend, to get him ready for the sacrifice . . .'

Crouching, John launched himself at Matthew. He locked an arm around his neck and dragged him backwards. Matthew sprawled on the floor on his back, shielding his face with his arm as John stood astride him, his fist raised. In an instant the Magister pulled him away.

'John . . . no! What are you thinking of? This is God's house. Hugh is lying there dead. Have you no respect?'

'Sir . . . he said . . . he said . . .'

'I heard what he said.' The Magister stood between them, his back to Matthew, and spoke in a low voice. 'You know Matthew. He didn't mean . . .'

'Oh yes he did. He meant it. And you believe the Jews are guilty too. You're all the same. All of you . . . all of you . . .'

He broke free and ran, hobbling, down to the west door. For a second time, the Magister made no attempt to stop him.

A blast of noise swept in as he opened it. Outside, the mob was massing together, brandishing pitchforks, rakes, knives, hammers, anything they could lay hands on to use as a weapon. Inside, Canon Humphrey, kneeling beside the body of Canon Senan, looked round, his face anxious. Another canon came over to John.

'Outside or in, make up your mind. But close this door.'

As the door clicked to behind him, John faced a forest of backs. The crowd was facing away from the cathedral. The shadows of the twin towers stretched outside across the square but it seemed that, rather than gathering the people in, they were pointing the way across the square towards the path to the Jew's house. Dotted about through the mob, men were standing on boxes or on stalls, whipping up the crowd to fever pitch. Among them, John thought he saw the pedlar, a long fork in his hand, punching it into the air.

John snaked along between the people, heading across to the end of the square where he could see down into Aaron's garden. There was no smoke coming from the chimney, the shutters were closed and nothing moved, but coming up the path from the city was another mob, howling, brandishing makeshift weapons. John could hear the same words ripping out into the air: 'Hang them . . . down with the Jews . . . sacrifice . . . murderers . . . evil magic . . . heathens . . .' From the roof of the gatehouse in the city wall a horn was blaring the alarm, echoed by another, further back along the hillside.

Useless to try to warn Reuben and Aaron. John could not reach them and they must know, must hear what was happening even from inside the little stone house with the shutters closed. But how to stop this rabble from breaking in, stringing them up . . .

As John watched, helpless, the two great tides of people began to converge on the pathway, spilling on to the slippery, frost-tipped grass on the hillside, sliding about trying to get a foothold, as those above careered down over the edge of the escarpment on to those trying to climb up. The howls turned to screams as men fell, some of them on to their weapons. Bodies rolled or were trampled underfoot as those in front yelled for the people behind to stop.

John spun round at the sound of hooves behind him. Across the square came a posse of men, the Earl's men, his arms emblazoned on their chests. At the top of the escarpment, some dismounted and continued down the hill on foot. Others reined in their horses till they reared, then zig-zagged down the frozen turf, the horses whinnying and tossing their heads at the pull on the bit as the riders held them back against the steep drop. The crowd began to panic, running this way and that to avoid the high-stepping animals with their rolling eyes. The shouts for blood turned to cries of fear as the people scattered, dropping their weapons.

Gradually John realized the soldiers were rounding up the people, controlling them, deliberately hurting no one but quietening them as they gathered, sullen and muttering, a little way from Reuben's house. A soldier removed his helmet, and John saw it was the Earl's steward.

'Be quiet! Silence! Listen all of you,' he bawled, holding up his arms. When the murmurs died down, he went on in a lower voice that still carried through the frosty air to John, lying on his belly now, out of sight, but listening and watching from the top of the hill.

'Listen . . . My friends . . . My lord feels as you do. The murder of the child Hugh was a terrible deed and will be paid for . . . believe me, it will be paid for. But there will be no murder done here today.'

A mutinous snarl broke out among the suspicious crowd.

'An eye for an eye . . .'

'They need 'angin' an' we'll do it . . .'

'They're in there now . . . let's go . . .'

A small group broke away and swarmed towards the house but two soldiers, their swords drawn, barred the way. John held his breath. The Earl's steward looked down at them then back at the crowd.

'My lord understands and shares your anger and you will have your revenge – but the right way . . . the way of the law . . .'

Another growl ran through the crowd.

'The way of the law, I said. We have come to arrest

Reuben ben Ezra, the Jew. You know he is the leader of the Jews in the city and is responsible for them. He will be tried according to the law. It is the Earl's wish . . .'

More angry cries broke out.

'It is the Earl's wish . . . and . . . it is the King's wish,' said the steward, raising his voice.

The crowd seemed to draw back a little and a whisper started round.

'The King . . . ? Why the King . . . ?'

'Don't worry, my friends,' said the steward. 'His Majesty is also aware of the ways of these Jews and hates them as much as you. They are indeed heathens and money-lenders. My lord and the King have known that for a long time. But His Majesty is gracious and merciful. Even in the face of this heinous crime, their leader Reuben ben Ezra is to be given a fair trial . . .'

'And found guilty!' yelled a voice.

The steward let out a great laugh. 'Oh, found guilty no doubt,' he said and the mood of the crowd changed in an instant. They began to bang on the ground with their pitchforks and sticks, chanting and cat-calling.

'Arrest him – arrest him – arrest him . . .'

'Go in and get him,' said the steward to the soldiers with the drawn swords. 'Break down the door if you have to.'

'Break down the door,' intoned the crowd, 'break down the door . . .'

The steward wheeled his horse in front of the gate. Before the soldiers could enter, the door opened and

Reuben came out. His head high, he walked slowly down the path, his hands folded calmly in front of him. A soldier pushed back the gate and he stepped through. He looked up at the steward.

'There will be no broken doors,' he said. 'I am here of my own free will. I have no fear of a trial. I am an innocent man.'

The steward's horse pranced and wheeled, lifting polished hooves. He reined her in and glanced down at Reuben, raising an eyebrow.

'We shall see,' he said. He nodded down the hill towards the city. 'You will be held in the gatehouse for now and taken to the jail later. Along with any others of your tribe who give us trouble.'

'We have never given trouble,' said Reuben. 'In fact, as you know very well, we have never done anything but give – our assistance,' and he fixed the steward with unwavering eyes. 'Our valuable assistance.'

A flush of anger crossed the steward's face. He turned to a soldier and jerked his head towards Reuben. 'Tie him up,' he said, roughly.

The soldier took a rope wound round the pommel of his saddle and went towards Reuben. Reuben lifted his hands out of the way.

'There is no need,' he said. 'I will go with you. I do not need to be tied up like a criminal.'

But at a nod from the steward, the soldier wound the rope tightly round his wrists, then gave it a single turn round his neck. The crowd cheered and started to gather missiles to throw at the prisoner. With a hefty tug, the soldier started off down the hill, leading Reuben like a tethered beast, the rope cutting into his neck, making him hurry and stumble as the mud, stones and muck came flying through the air at him. The soldier gave a roar as a lump of frozen earth hit him by accident, but the crowd roared even louder in glee. A stone knocked off Reuben's hat and the crowd went wild as the soldier picked it up and jammed it on his own head, looking back at Reuben and raising two fingers at him.

Slowly the rest of the Earl's party moved forward, some of the horses shielding Reuben a little from the crowd. They followed, turning the cavalcade into a dreadful parody of the good-natured junketing of the Feast of Fools parade.

Could that have been only yesterday? John sat up, his elbows on his knees, pressing his hands to his face to stop them shaking as he watched the lonely figure of Reuben dragged along, hatless, through the city streets below to the doorway of the gatehouse, where, with a last torrent of projectiles and abuse, he was taken inside and the crowd slowly dispersed.

John stood up. He looked at the cathedral and then down at the house. He should go back to the mass for Hugh. But the most important thing he could do for Hugh now was to find out who had killed him. Others could, and would, say prayers. So would he, but later. And maybe the angel was watching over Hugh . . . or Saint Nicholas or Saint Hugh himself . . . but Aaron was down there frightened and alone. And if John could find the killer, then Reuben would be set free. John was sure that was what Hugh would want more than prayers.

There must be another reason for the two deaths and whoever did it knew the whole town wanted rid of the Jews – even the King it seemed – and was taking advantage . . . Reuben was just – just handy to take the blame. Like killing two birds with one stone.

'Huh,' he said to himself, with an ironic little smile, 'not funny.'

But perhaps someone thought it was. If only he knew where to start. Why would anyone want to kill Hugh? Perhaps he could understand killing Canon Senan, he did have enemies . . . but not Hugh . . . And yet the two deaths so close together couldn't just be by chance surely . . . there must be some connection if only he could find it. For the moment, Reuben's arrest seemed to be the only clue. Perhaps the Canon's and Reuben's special enemies were one and the same. And maybe . . . maybe Aaron at least knew who his father's might be . . .

John hurried down the path and in through the gate. The door was still half-open. Inside he could hear a low keening. He knocked but there was no reply. He pushed the door gently and he heard a quick gasp and a scrabbling noise as if someone was standing up quickly.

'Please,' he said, 'I won't hurt you. I'm not one of them . . .'

The open door cast a pool of light into the centre of the room. He went inside and waited while his eyes got used to the darkness in the corners. A figure was huddled against the wall.

'I'm John . . . Peg – Aaron's friend. Where is he?'

The figure moved forward a little out of the shadows. A woman stood there, her hair covered in a veil, the skirt of her long, dark gown huddled up against her with one hand and the fingers of the other pressed to her mouth.

'Please,' said John, 'it's all right.'

He suddenly remembered.

'Sha – shalom,' he said, 'shalom – a-aleikhem. Truly. I won't hurt you.'

The woman seemed to relax a little.

'Please,' said John, slowly, 'where is Aaron?'

The woman said nothing, but at the word Aaron, involuntarily, her eyes glanced towards the ceiling. John looked round. There were no stairs, but a narrow passageway opened out of the room. He started towards it and the woman immediately stood in front of it, her arms outstretched to the wall on either side. She let out a cry.

'Are you Aaron's mother?' said John.

She said nothing, but looked a question, her big, dark eyes, so like Aaron's, watching him with distrust.

John held out his hands. 'Look, I have no weapons. Nothing. I haven't come to hurt him – or you – or anyone. I just want to . . .'

There was a movement in the passageway behind her.

'Aaron? Aaron, is that you? It's me . . . Peg . . .'

There was a quick little laugh from the darkness. Then Aaron's voice, speaking in Hebrew. His mother turned and Aaron came out of the dark and stood beside her. Her arm went around his

169

shoulders and she held him close. More Hebrew and she began to relax. With a quick look outside, she closed the door and rammed a huge wooden bolt across, then went to a back window and opened the shutter a little so light filtered in. She pulled out a chair for John and they sat round the table at one side of the room.

'Peg, you shouldn't be here,' said Aaron.

'You sound like your father,' said John, 'and like the Magister and . . .'

'Well, you shouldn't,' said Aaron, but with a smile. Then he frowned. 'But I'm sorry too . . . I'm so sorry about – about Hugh. He was your friend, wasn't he?'

John nodded. No words came. He tightened his jaw and blinked hard, once, twice. He would not think about that still figure in the cathedral with the curls poking from the shroud and the hands crossed . . . the hands . . .

'What about your father?' he said abruptly. 'What are we going to do?'

'My father is innocent. He will stand trial and he will be found innocent,' said Aaron.

'You believe that?'

'Of course. Isn't it so?'

'It's so that he's innocent. I believe it but no one else will. I've heard them out there. And I think . . . I'm sure . . . there is at least one person out there who wants him to be guilty.'

Aaron nodded. 'I suppose so. My father has for some time warned me to be careful. I don't understand why, but I know that it is true that we are hated. And it's easier for the gentiles if it is one of us that's guilty.' He fingered the yellow badge on his arm.

John gave him a watery grin. 'Marked men,' he said. 'Huh. No, I mean that someone wants your father blamed to protect themselves. Aaron, do you know who it might be?'

Aaron shook his head.

'I don't know your Christian ways,' he said, 'and I don't know all the people my father knows . . . not yet. I am learning about his dealings but . . .' He shook his head again.

'Any of the others? The other Jews in the city?'

'They all live close to us here. I doubt they know more than we do. My father is the leader. I don't know what will happen now.'

He turned to his mother and spoke in Hebrew. She shook her head.

'No,' said Aaron. 'There are many, many people in the city who owe us money. It could have been anyone.'

'Money . . . you think someone owed you so much that they couldn't pay, so . . . that's terrible. To kill Hugh because . . . because . . .'

John dropped his head on to his arms, leaning on the table. So much hatred and greed was more than he could deal with. After a moment he looked up, ran his hands back over his head, then placed them firmly side by side on the table.

'One thing is certain then – if I don't find out who killed him, your father will be hanged. At least my – my father's death was an – an accident, but I know what it's like to be without him. Hugh is dead too, and for what? Well, they won't either of them be back, but your father's still alive and at least I can try and keep it so.' He smiled at Aaron. 'So the best I can do is go and get on with it . . .'

'I'll come with you.'

'No. It's too dangerous for you. They'll put you in the gatehouse with him.'

'So be it. At least I would have tried too.'

'Aaron. You can't disappear into the crowd like I can. Your clothes. Your hat. Your yellow badge.'

'Your foot.'

'You know what I mean. I'm just one of them . . . marked maybe, but one of them. I can go and come anywhere – just a chorister. A Christian. Not you. But I'll come and tell you what I find. I'll come at night, when everyone's asleep.'

'And the watch?'

'I've got past them before, and I will again.'

With a little grin, Aaron turned and explained everything to his mother, still sitting anxiously beside him.

'My mother says she will leave the shutter off the side window. Just tap on the glass and we'll come. I'll sleep down here. And she says – thank you . . .'

John nodded, stood up and went to the door. He heaved back the heavy bolt and peered outside.

'All clear. I daresay they're all at the gatehouse throwing stones at the door,' he said, closing his eyes briefly, shaking his head. 'They're all so stupid . . .'

'My father says stupidity often wins,' said Aaron.

'Not while I'm alive,' said John, and with a quick smile, was gone.

Chapter 15

' 'Course 'e'll be guilty. Guilty as Old Nick.'

'Slippery them Jews . . .'

John walked a little way behind two men crossing the square, straining to hear but trying to look as if he wasn't in the least interested in what they were saying.

'Listen, even if 'e ain't guilty – an' 'oo else is it – but even if 'e ain't, they got ways of makin' 'em confess down in that jail. Ye can 'ear 'em screamin' for miles.'

'True.'

He rubbed his hands, happily.

'Leave it to the lads down there. 'E'll be got down there today, you'll see. They only took 'im to the gate'ouse to get 'im out of the way quick. Dunno why 'e's got to 'ave a fair trial, but 'e 'as, so that's that.'

'D'you reckon 'e done fer old Canon Thunderguts too?'

'Aye, there's that. Dunno about 'im. Coulda been anyone. But 'oever done fer *im* deserves a pension. Miserable ole bastard. We're well rid of 'im.'

'We'll be well rid of the Jew too.'

'Well. Yeh. 'Cept, 'oo do the rich bastards get money off if not 'im? And if the rich bastards got no money, then we ain't neither.'

The man shrugged and slapped his hands against his sides. His friend nodded sagely, his rat-grey hair slithering backwards and forwards on his red-veined cheeks, and they vanished into a clutch of shacks at the far side of the square beyond the canons' houses. John slipped into the cathedral.

For a moment he stood in the shadows. It would soon be curfew. There were few people about and it was quiet. Canon Humphrey no longer knelt with Canon Senan's body; another priest had taken his place. He was supposed to be praying, but had dozed off, leaning against the doorway of the shrine. The mass for Hugh had ended too. There would be more during the night and next day, but someone should be with him, kneeling, praying, keeping watch, and John could see no one.

He went a little closer. Close to Hugh's head, a single candle burned, leaving a tide of darkness round about him. Then, sprawled in the shadows on the floor on the far side of Hugh, John noticed a figure in red. Another canon gone to sleep. But as he moved round a little closer, he saw one of the man's hands clutch convulsively at the binding of Hugh's shroud. Great sobs shook the body and the fist of the other hand was stuffed into the mouth, chewing at the knuckles. The closed eyelids were wet and sore with little patches of flaking skin. Every few moments, the eyes opened wide, unseeing, as the man took great gasps of air from the side of his mouth.

Canon Gwyllim.

John drew back quickly behind a column. This was far, far more than watching over the dead. The man had collapsed. Was he ill? Or . . . was this grief, grief that had almost prostrated him . . . Was he the one . . . the one Hugh had said he had to watch out for . . . the one that Hugh had kept at arm's length. Grief? Or guilt? Suppose Canon Gwillym had put Hugh in the cabin in the wood so that he could force him to . . . John shuddered. Forced him and then killed him so he would say nothing? This at last might be a reason for Hugh's death.

Footsteps came hurrying from the vestry. John edged a little further round the column out of sight.

'What are you doing, man? Get up, get up, for God's sake. You are making an exhibition of yourself.'

Canon Humphrey strode up to the bier and pulled at Canon Gwillym's shoulder.

'Go, for God's sake. I will stay here and watch. Go home and pull yourself together. If my lord Bishop hears of this . . . you know how he feels about . . . get up, will you . . .'

'I – I c-c-an't . . . he was . . . he was . . .'

'Shut up!' He clamped a hand over the Canon's slobbering mouth, then snatched it away, wiping it down his robe. 'Ugh! Mother of God, give me strength. Sweet Jesu, help me get him out of here.'

He heaved at the bloated, inert body on the floor and finally hauled the Canon to his feet, where he stood swaying and weeping, his pink face swollen and his hands trembling. Canon Humphrey grabbed his arm, pulled it round his own neck, and supported him, tottering and reeling, choking and retching, across the nave and into the vestry.

John crept over to the bier. He looked at the pierced hands and then at the closed eyes that would never laugh with him again. So many nevers. So many . . . He must not think. He knelt down.

'Hugh? Was it him? Was it Canon Gwyllim?' he said in a low, fierce voice. 'Why, oh why can't you tell me . . . ? But I'll find out. I will. I promise you.' He looked up at the last angel overhead, then back at Hugh. 'I promise you,' he said again. 'I'll find out somehow . . . and that's all I can do.'

He stood up and hurried away round the apse to come at the vestry door from behind. Any minute Canon Humphrey would go to take over the watch at Hugh's side. He would go back the way he had come without passing John. And when he did . . .

The vestry door opened. Canon Humphrey came out and looked back inside.

'Gwyllim? Answer me. You will go home? Now?'

A sound came that might have been a muffled 'yes', and with a snort and an irritable shake of his head, Canon Humphrey composed himself and, head lowered and hands together, walked slowly over to Hugh, knelt down and crossed himself. He would be there a long time.

John turned the handle of the vestry door as quietly as he could. It creaked a little as he opened it, but across the nave, Canon Humphrey did not move. John slid inside and closed it behind him.

Canon Gwyllim was sitting on a stool, tears still

trickling down his cheeks, still taking gulps of air, but calmer now, little shudders racking him, rocking gently from side to side. He looked at John but made no attempt to dry his eyes or to be still. He did not even seem surprised to see him there.

'Canon Gwyllim . . . sir . . .'

The Canon shook his head and waved a hand vaguely in the air as if willing John to vanish. John crouched beside him, wondering how to start.

'Hugh . . . Hugh was my friend . . .'

A fresh storm of weeping broke out. Canon Gwyllim bowed his head almost to his lap and his shoulders shook.

'Sir . . .' John looked round at the door anxiously. 'Sir . . . you've got to stop. Please listen . . . I must know . . .'

He put both hands on the Canon's shoulders and shoved him upright, taking his weight. The man turned his head to one side but made no attempt to push John away. He almost seemed to welcome him, leaning heavily on him. John gave another heave and propped him against the wall, where he slumped, his eyes closed, exhausted.

'Sir . . . please, I must know. Canon Gwyllim, can you hear me?'

A faint nod.

'Did you – did you . . . kill Hugh?'

Slowly the Canon's eyes opened and a puzzled frown came over his face.

'Kill . . . Hugh?' His lips trembled and he tried to shake his head, but it was too much for him. 'Kill him? Kill him! I – I l-l-lo—'

'If that's what you call it,' said John, breaking in angrily. 'Did you hound him, and hound him, and then, when you were drunk after the feast, hide him in the woods so you could . . . could . . . and then kill him because he might tell . . . ? Did you?'

Suddenly, John's anger seemed to sweep through the Canon, taking him over. He tore John's hand from his shoulder, put a hand on the table and pulled himself to his feet, breathing heavily, scornful eyes raking John from head to foot.

'What would you know, you ugly little cripple? No one will ever feel like that about you. Not like that. He was – he was perfect . . . and I never touched a hair of his head,' he said, threatening to burst into tears again, his mouth quivering.

'Only because he was too quick for you,' said John. 'That's what he said.'

The Canon gave a humourless little smile.

'Did he? Well . . .'

He looked down at John.

'I didn't touch him. Ever. Not once. And I didn't kill him. It was the Jews,' he said. 'We all know that.'

'Not all of us,' said John, standing up.

The Canon gathered himself together and went to the outside door.

'It was the Jews,' he said again, pulling it open. 'Best to leave it like that. The Jews . . .'

He stumbled out into the night, wiping his face on his sleeve. Outside, the cold air seemed to sober him and he waddled away towards his house, rubbing at his clothes with his hands as if trying to clean off something dirty.

'No,' said John, quietly, watching him. 'Ugly little cripple I may be, but I won't leave it like that. You know something, Canon Gwyllim. I believe you didn't kill Hugh, though God knows you're capable, but I think you know who did.'

Chapter 16

As John pushed open the door of the dormitory, Edward Longnose came down the stairs.

'Going to the midden,' he called out over his shoulder as he came. At the bottom, he took John by the arm and hurried him outside.

'I've been listening out for you. Best not to come in,' he said.

'Matthew?' said John.

'And the rest. But it's Matthew really. He's got them believing you are in league with the Jews and the devil and all else . . . He's trying to say you had a hand in killing Hugh and the Canon.'

'Edward – why should they believe that? Why would I kill Hugh . . . or anyone? But listen, if I don't come in . . . it'll look as if I've got something to hide . . . they'll believe it even more.'

Edward shook his head. 'The Magister's not here and I don't answer for . . .'

'The way he is, he wouldn't do anything anyway.'

'That's not fair. He wouldn't let them . . .'

From upstairs came the sound of droning and chanting.

'What in the world are they doing?' said John.

'Matthew's got them making spells against you. He took candles from the vestry and they've made wax dolls that—'

'That's witchcraft! He's worse than I'm supposed to be.'

Edward nodded and crossed himself. 'It's nothing to what he'll make them do if you turn up.'

'Does the Magister know?'

'I don't think so, else he'd be here. He wouldn't let them do all that stuff either.'

He jerked a thumb upwards. John heaved a quick sigh.

'Well, that's another night in the cold for me, then,' he said. 'Thanks for the warning.'

'I don't know the rights and wrongs of it all,' said Edward, doubtfully, 'and I've got to live with them upstairs, but I don't reckon you're in league with anyone. Still . . . I reckon it was the Jews killed Hugh though, Peg.'

He glanced at John.

'I just don't think you had anything to do with it. But you've been seen with them, Peg, and you shouldn't be. Speaking a word to them's one thing, but we shouldn't mix with them – it's the law. So be careful.'

John gave a curt nod. 'Think what you like,' he said gruffly, 'but they didn't kill Hugh any more than I did. But I'm beginning to get an idea of who did.'

He frowned. His eyes went to the dormitory stairs and the dreary noise coming from above.

'You mean Matthew?'

'Well . . . Let's say he's mixed up in it somehow,

even if he didn't . . . didn't do it. He's got a lot to answer for. Maybe I should come in and—'

'No,' said Edward. 'There's too many of them. They'll all turn on you. I know they will.'

He seemed suddenly panicky.

'I'd best get back up there or they'll get suspicious,' he said. John nodded. 'Yes. I understand. Thanks, Edward. But tomorrow . . .'

'Get Matthew when he's on his own then. I must go.'

Edward vanished into the dark interior of the dormitory and John heard someone greet him as he went up the stairs. Then he heard Matthew's voice, strident and full of malice.

He turned back into the night. Where to go? With the masses for the dead going on, there were too many clerics about in the cathedral for it to be safe there. They would ask questions. He thought of Rufus's warm kitchen, but earlier, Rufus hadn't wanted him there. He heard the watch calling the hour from the city wall below, the thin voice crackling through the air. Another would be tramping round the square soon, checking that the curfew was kept.

The nearest clump of bushes was at the top of the path down to the city. Hugging the walls, he circled the dormitory house till he was facing them, then, crouching low, he scurried across the cobbles, trying to keep his clogs as quiet as he could. He swore quietly as he slipped on a patch of ice. With a quick look back across the deserted square, he ducked down out of sight. As he began to crawl forward, a hand grasped his gown and tugged it.

Heart pounding and fists raised, he spun round and almost fell as his foot gave way. A pair of hands caught him.

'Thank God I've found you.'

'Aaron! What – why are you here?' He steadied himself, then pulled Aaron after him into the prickly undergrowth. 'I said *I'd* come to *you*. You shouldn't be out. Your mother . . .'

'She is asleep. Well, I hope she is asleep. Anyway, she's upstairs and I was very quiet. I had to find you. Peg, it's worse, far worse than I thought.'

'Yes?'

'They are going to torture my father, to make him confess.'

John dropped his chin on his chest, sighed, and looked up. 'Yes . . . I wasn't going to tell you.'

'You knew?'

'I – I just heard a rumour. Old men talking. But I thought it might be true. I didn't want your mother – or you – to know.'

'You're wrong. I should know. I am head of my family while my father is away. And I must do something about it.'

'Aaron. There is only one thing to be done and that's find the killer. Now listen . . .'

He wriggled about and broke back a couple of branches so they could sit more easily and think. A flurry of ice fell on their faces and they brushed it away.

'I've been trying to work it out. Which of them could have done it?'

'Not my father. Nor any of us.'

'I know that, you don't need to tell me. So who? There's the canons.'

'But they're religious men . . .' Aaron sounded horrified.

'Huh, not so's you'd notice – well, I suppose some of them are, but a lot aren't, believe me. I've been thinking and thinking, and the only reason I can come up with is that Hugh saw Canon Senan killed and then he was killed to stop him talking. Then it was easy to make the – the marks on his hands so everyone would think it was your people that crucified him. I just hope . . . I just hope he was dead when – when they did it . . .'

He shuddered, screwing up his own hands into tight fists, digging the nails into his palms.

Aaron closed his eyes. 'Don't.' He swallowed and drew a deep breath. 'So . . . who would want to kill Canon Senan?'

'A lot of people,' said John. 'He'd had a row with Canon Gwyllim. I think that Canon Senan knew that he liked – liked Hugh a lot and that he told him it was evil and that he would tell the Bishop. It's only guessing, but I think it might have been something like that.'

'That's terrible.'

'Yes. But Canon Gwyllim says he didn't kill Hugh . . . and the way he talked about it . . . about Hugh, I think I believe him . . . but I can't be sure . . .'

He shook his head, frowning, then started again.

'Then there's money. D'you think Canon Senan knew who owed your father money and was going

184

to tell the Bishop about that? Canon Humphrey maybe – or anyone. There may be a lot of them.'

'I know there are. Peg, there are dozens.'

'Well there's a dozen more then, at least, who might have done it. Then there's the pedlar.'

'Pedlar?'

'The one who sells relics that aren't relics.'

'Oh . . . animal bones . . . yes, my father has told me about that.'

'The Canon threw him out of the cathedral. And Hugh was hidden in the wood, and the pedlar has a shack somewhere there so he probably knows the wood like the back of his hand . . .'

'Peg . . . it's like a maze . . . How do we find the end of the string that leads to the centre?'

John sighed again, putting his head on his knees. 'And – there's Matthew.'

'Matthew?'

'The boy that hates me. He hated Hugh too. But he didn't hate Canon Senan. At least I don't know any reason why he should. If anything he was always hanging round the canons, arse-licking – though I never saw him with Canon Senan himself, it's true.'

'Perhaps it was the other way round. Perhaps Matthew killed Hugh and the Canon found out, so Matthew killed him.'

John thought for a moment. He shook his head. 'No . . . no, that doesn't work. Hugh was alive when I saw him in the building in the wood.'

He thought of Hugh struggling to sit up and his hands on the ground in the patch of light.

'He didn't have the marks then either. And

Matthew didn't have time to take Hugh away and then go back to kill him later. Still, he did know that Canon Senan was holding Hugh's hair when he was found. And I don't know how he could have known that, unless the Magister . . . Aaron there's one thing certain. It wasn't the Magister. He was with us all the time.'

'At least that's something. Couldn't you ask him to help?'

'No. He believes your people are guilty and he is angry with me for talking to your father and for . . . oh, a lot of things. It doesn't matter, but he won't help unless I shove the answer straight under his nose.'

Aaron pushed his hand under his hat and scratched his head. Suddenly the cathedral bell started to toll. The masses were beginning again.

'Perhaps if I go in and just keep my ears open, someone will say something . . . let something drop . . . Whoever it was is likely to be there sometime during the day . . .'

'But they won't talk. Why should they?'

'If it's the pedlar, he might not, he's a loner, but the others are in each other's pockets . . . they jabber on about everything all the time, and in any case, they'll want to stoke up the rumours about your father.'

'I'd better get back. Peg, take care . . .'

'Don't worry.'

Cautiously, they parted the bushes and crawled out.

'You'd be safer going that way,' said John, pointing down the cascade over the rocks. 'No one would see you breaking the curfew if you climb down there. I'll help you. I've done it before, remember.'

Aaron shook his head. 'No, not that way,' he said firmly. 'I'll go the front way. That's the way my father would go.'

So he would.

'Find out who did it, Peg, find them,' said Aaron. 'And Peg . . . shalom . . .' and he gave him a swift hug.

With a wry little smile, John watched him hurry down the steps and in through the gate of his house. He raised a hand up towards John, though John knew he probably couldn't be seen against the bushes in the dark from that distance. Aaron went in and closed the door.

'The way my father would go . . .'

What about him? Was he going the way *his* father would go? His father would go for the truth, that was certain. The truth . . . that was the best he could do.

He burrowed back into the undergrowth and slept fitfully for a couple of hours, till he heard the door of the dormitory house open and the boys crossing the square.

He wouldn't join them in the vestry. He needed information, not confrontation. Better to go to the side chapels close to Hugh or Canon Senan, listening out for anything he could glean. He waited till the boys had gone and started across the square. As he went in through the west door, he reached up and gave his little carved ploughman a pat.

Inside, Canon Humphrey was saying mass for

Hugh. Forty or fifty people were already there, weeping, wailing, wringing their hands. On the far side of the nave, fewer mourners knelt with Canon Senan. John felt a twinge of pity at the lonely figure lying so still, a single candle shining down on to his white, chiselled face, all the rage ebbed away, leaving him tranquil at last. He looked as if he were made of stone, and a memory stirred in John's hands of the sensation of the tool cutting into the block, peeling away the outline of a jaw, the rasp of the file smoothing down the cool expanse of a marble cheek.

With a little start, he pulled himself together and looked round. He crossed himself and knelt down where he could see the people around the bier on which the Canon lay. From the corners of lowered eyes, he could see that there was no one there he thought might be suspicious, just one or two canons whose names he didn't know and some of the men choristers, no doubt nursing thick heads after the feast and maybe even feeling vaguely guilty that they were inside carousing while the Canon was outside being beaten to death. John stayed for a moment or two, then stood up to cross the nave to Hugh, now lying among a forest of candles.

He stood at the back of the crowd, reluctant to look at the body that seemed to get smaller each time he saw it. He swallowed hard and clamped his jaw together tightly. He would not cry. Crying would do nothing for Hugh and it would stop him thinking straight. He must keep his mind clear.

He peered through the crowd. Neither Canon Gwyllim nor Canon Humphrey was there, but in the front row the Earl was kneeling, his steward and several of his men beside him. The Earl was deathly pale and once or twice the steward had to support him as he swayed. After a while, he got to his feet, managed to genuflect at the foot of the bier, turned and, with the steward and his men surrounding him, stumbled away down the nave.

'He's a good young man,' John heard someone mutter. 'Look at him. Real upset about the little fella. 'E was with 'im night before . . .'

'Paid for all the candles,' said another. 'Mint o' money just burnin' away there . . .'

'Quite right too,' came the reply. ' 'E's a little martyr . . . crucified 'e was . . . them Jews . . .'

There was a stir in the aisle behind him. John looked round and quickly slipped behind a column. The pedlar was hurrying along amid a bunch of dirty, tattered men and women, their fingers like talons, their hair matted, their feet wrapped in rags. The pedlar's arm was round the shoulder of an old man whose eyes were covered with a filthy bandage. His arms were stretched before him, clawing the air, as the pedlar half-carried, half-dragged him along.

'Make way, make way.'

The crowd drew back before the urgent cries of the pedlar. He pushed through to the feet of the bier and lowered the old man to the ground, his grisly-looking companions crowding round him. The crowd drew back even further at the stench they gave off, but watched avidly, always eager for the next sensation. John edged forward through the crowd. The priest taking the mass hesitated. Before he could intervene, the pedlar took the old man's hands, placed them on the bier and whispered to him. The old man scrabbled about, then found Hugh's arm and hooked his crooked, grasping fingers into the bands of the shroud.

'Little martyr,' he said, his voice high and quavering, 'little martyr, have mercy on me. Give me my sight . . . give me my sight . . .'

The priest stood up, raising his hands. 'My son,' he said, and stopped, still uncertain, casting round for someone to tell him what to do.

Again the old man spoke. 'Please, little martyr . . . I long to see you . . . let me see you . . . give me my eyes . . .'

He started to grovel and moan, laying his filthy head on his hands, spittle running down his chin and on to the pall covering the bier. John itched to rush forward and pull him away but suddenly the old man gave a great cry and the crowd gasped. The pedlar steadied him, unfastened the bandage round his eyes and stood back. The crowd, silent now, was spellbound. The old man passed his hands over his face, feeling it with his fingertips. Then he raised his head, his eyes closed, and struggled to his feet. He kept his eyes screwed up against the light of the candles, then slowly he opened them, flickering and trembling.

'I can see! I can see! God be praised . . .'

John watched him turn to face the crowd, his eyes wide and staring, blinking just a little, turning his head this way and that as if seeing everything for the first time. Instantly, they fell to their knees. His face wrinkled into a blissful smile, showing blackened teeth and gums.

'God be praised!'

His voice trumpeted out powerfully, much stronger than might be expected for an old and ailing man. But a miracle was a miracle. The people joined in his shouts of triumph.

'God be praised!'

'A miracle!'

'We have a new saint . . . a martyr . . . our own martyr . . .'

The pedlar embraced the old man and led him round the crowd for them to touch him, to kiss his hand, to marvel. Quickly, John drew back behind the column in case the pedlar should see him, in case he should have to kiss that disgusting claw.

'Truly,' the pedlar said to the priest, 'we have a miracle 'ere today.' He nodded sanctimoniously, crossing himself. 'And I've been – honoured – to play my humble part in it. Thanks be to Christ Jesu and that blessed child that lies there, a martyr and soon to be a saint, if right is done . . .'

He fixed the priest with an unwavering eye. The priest, bewildered, gave a hurried blessing to the old man and to the crowd and looked relieved as Canon Humphrey hurried across from the vestry.

'What is this? What is going on? What has happened?'

'Canon Humphrey,' said the priest, 'it is this good man here. He was blind . . . he could see nothing when he came in . . . but when he touched the poor crucified child here, the chorister . . . they took off the bandage and he could see.'

Canon Humphrey said nothing but looked from the pedlar to the old man and back again, running his tongue over his teeth, sucking in his cheeks. John could see he was carefully weighing up the situation.

'Come here, old man,' said the Canon eventually. 'Is this true?'

The old man was still passing among the excited crowd like royalty.

'True as I'm standin' 'ere,' said the pedlar. 'It's a true miracle at the 'ands of that martyred child there.' He nodded towards Hugh but directed his gaze at Canon Humphrey through narrowed eyes.

Canon Humphrey looked back at him and pursed his lips. 'I asked the old man, my son. Let him answer for himself.'

The crowd pointed the old man towards the Canon.

'Look,' said someone. 'See for yourself, Canon Humphrey, sir. Look at him.'

His hands clasped to his chest and singularly light of step, the old man went to the Canon. His face was . . . beatific. His eyes, though faded with age, seemed to have a glow, a sparkle even, as he gazed upwards.

'See,' he said, 'I can even see them angels up there flyin' about in 'eaven. God be praised.'

Together, the crowd sighed. John felt a flash of anger at the mention of the angels. They had nothing to do with this old man and his lies, for lies he was sure they were.

Canon Humphrey pursed his mouth again. 'Yes. I

see. Old man, you must come with me. We must take you to the Bishop. We need to . . .'

The pedlar laid a proprietorial hand on the old man's arm. 'I'll come with yer,' he said. 'Ye will need a friend to – to keep a lookout for yer . . .'

In vain, Canon Humphrey protested. The pedlar locked his arm into the old man's and with his other hand held on tightly to the bandage, holding it up for everyone to see, they went into the vestry.

'Another relic,' thought John, as the crowd jostled and fought for a view, some rushing to spread the news outside in the square or down in the city, some shouldering their way towards the closed door of the vestry, others milling about babbling on about miracles, and a very few returning to pray.

'At least it's taken their minds off Reuben ben Ezra,' thought John. 'How could they have believed all that rubbish. Hugh's lying there dead and . . .'

He turned away quickly.

'Anyone could say they were blind and pull off a bandage like that,' he said, muttering to himself. 'Hugh's not a saint.'

'He's good for trade,' said a quiet voice beside him.

John looked up. The Earl's steward gave him a wink and walked on, his brilliant, elegant clothes fluttering behind him.

Chapter 17

John was exhausted and his mind was churning. Surely, surely, no one would have killed Hugh just to make a saint of him for money. He thought of the old man scrabbling at Hugh's dead arm, gazing up at the angels with that fake holy look in his eyes, and felt sick. All that miracle business just complicated things further and he was no nearer finding the killer.

And Reuben's trial was tomorrow.

He slumped against a rock in Canon Humphrey's garden. Between thoughts, he gnawed half-heartedly at a bone, a mug of ale at his feet. Rufus was a bit more friendly now. The cook had recovered his temper and given him food to give to John, but it was back to scraps from the bucket – for which he was truly thankful – and he had to eat it outside.

'Cook still ain't up to visitors,' Rufus had said with feeling, rubbing his backside. That didn't matter, it was safer outside; you could see better who you could trust out here.

The frost was beginning to melt and great black clouds were massing over the cathedral. Rain. Not yet, but soon. John had nowhere to go but he couldn't just sit there. He got up, emptied the dregs on the path and reached in to shove the empty mug through the kitchen door. Rufus snatched it in passing and waved him away with a glance at the cook, who looked up, glowered at him and gave an extra hearty whack with his cleaver at a great joint of raw beef. John left quickly, wiping his hands down his robe.

Inside the cathedral, bedlam still reigned from the west door right up the nave to the chapel where Hugh lay. A ring of priests stood round him to keep the throng at bay. Another, looking nervous, droned out the mass at breakneck speed and the crowd joined in, ecstatic and hysterical. John shook his head in disgust and went into the apse, to Saint Aelred's shrine, deserted in favour of a new marvel.

Hearing voices, he drew back quickly into the shelter of a column. Matthew was there, talking to someone else he couldn't see. Matthew's voice sounded high-pitched and agitated. A second, older voice sounded angry.

'Be quiet, will you!'

John tried to edge nearer.

'But I'm glad you did it,' said Matthew, 'I'm glad.'

'Will you shut it?' said the other voice, hissing out the words. 'Or must I make you . . .'

John was certain he had heard the voice before but couldn't place it. Where had he heard it . . . where?

'But I'm on your side,' said Matthew, whining. 'That's why I—'

'Shut it, I said.'

There was a sudden silence.

'Someone's back there. They may have heard.

Look, there's a shadow . . . get after him, you fool.'

John wasted no time. He shook off his clogs and ran as fast as he could back into the crowd, trying to lose himself, buffeting into people, worming between them, stumbling over kneeling legs, trampling on feet with his own injured foot. Behind him he heard shouting and protests as Matthew blundered after him. Down the nave he went, heads turning, mouths opening, hands clutching at him. He tore himself free and barged between outstretched arms, elbowing one man in the stomach and sending him flying.

Halfway down the nave, ahead of him he heard a crash. Someone had slammed the west door to block his way out. Too late to get back to the vestry. He turned. Matthew was closing the gap. The crowd was agog. Twisting back on himself, he made for the door to the tower.

Pointing behind him, he jumped up and down and yelled, 'Look there! Look! Look out!'

As one, the crowd looked round. John slipped through the door and shut it before they could turn back and see where he'd gone. He scrambled up a few steps, stumbled and stopped.

Total darkness. Slowly, he crawled up a little further, feeling his way, till gradually his eyes became accustomed to the dim, patchy light filtering in through the slits in the outer wall. Holding his breath, he waited. He might have fooled the crowd, but had Matthew seen him come in? The answer came as down below he heard the door open and close, letting in a spurt of the din from the mob.

Well, Matthew wasn't used to this place like he

was. John crept on up the stairs, his hand against the inner wall of the spiral. Below him, he heard Matthew stumble and curse, hampered by his clogs, but he didn't stop. Without his clogs, John had the advantage of silence. He paused at the bell room, but the single window there let in light and there was nowhere to hide and no door. On he went, an idea forming in his head. If only the cell above were open and the key in the lock . . .

Up he went, higher and higher. Below, he heard Matthew stop at the bell room, then start climbing again. John turned into the narrow passage to the cell. The door was ajar, opening inwards. John darted past it to the far side, round a bend in the passage, where he flattened himself against the wall and waited. Matthew came panting up the stairs. He paused, listening, then put a hand on the massive door frame and leant forward, peering into the blackness. John was too far round the turning to get back and push him inside without giving himself away.

'Go on, go inside . . . please . . .'

John closed his eyes for a second, willing Matthew to go into the cell. Matthew stood still, rubbing his fists on his legs, breathing heavily, then slowly and hesitantly, keeping one hand in contact with the open door, he went into the room. John crept into the doorway behind him. Matthew still had hold of the huge, iron door-handle but he was leaning forward, groping into the dark with the other hand. With one quick, mighty blow, John sent him sprawling. He heaved on the door, but Matthew's legs were in the way, jamming it open. With his good foot, John kicked and kicked till Matthew, screaming, twisted his legs up out of the way. John heaved again, his thin shoes slipping on the stone, but the door swung to and slammed, the noise echoing down the stairs. Through the tiny, barred hatch, he heard Matthew scrabbling towards the door. Quickly, he felt for the keyhole.

The key wasn't there. Grimly, he hung on to the handle, his other hand searching the wood and the iron studs. At last he found the bolt. With a deep breath, he took hold of it, turned it into position and rammed it home. Breathless and sweating, he leant against the door.

'Let me out, you bastard . . . you gimp . . . let me out . . .'

Matthew hammered on the door. John shot home the second bolt.

'I'll let you out when you tell the truth about Hugh. I'm going for help.'

The hammering grew less.

'No, don't leave me up here . . . please . . . please . . . I hate the dark . . . I'll tell you anything . . . I'll . . . I'll . . . please . . .'

John wiped his sleeve over his forehead, sniffed and started back along the passage to the stairs, crabwise, his legs feeling weak, his back against the wall. He stopped. In the darkness he could hear someone coming up towards him.

He froze.

Whoever it was, was taking their time. The footsteps were even, unhurried, inexorable. Someone friendly, even the Magister, would call out, surely. It must be the man by the shrine and that man must have killed Hugh.

John went on up the stairs a little way, any sound he made covered by Matthew still pounding, albeit faintly now, on the cell door. The footsteps came on and on. They turned into the passageway and stopped at the cell door.

'Please . . . let me out,' said Matthew, choking and pleading.

With a grunt, the man drew back the bolt and John heard the door squeak open. He heard Matthew sobbing, and a deeper voice, low but hard and incisive, giving orders. Suddenly, he heard a slap.

Matthew cried out, his voice rising almost to a scream, 'All right, all right. I'll do it.'

Do what?

Matthew's blubbing might cover him while he got past the passage opening and down the stairs first. John started downward, slipped and scrambled back.

Too late. The man was already at the entrance to the passage, looking up the stairs. He made a grab for John's leg but missed. John whipped round and was up and out of sight before the man could try again. The passageway to the rose window and across to the south tower was ahead. If he could get up there and down the other side . . .

Up and up he went, his chest sore and heaving and his foot aching and clumsy. The footsteps followed relentlessly, not hurrying, as if the man had all the time in the world.

John turned into the passageway. The archway

ahead was so narrow the man might not get through if he was as big as John thought he might be from his tread. He grabbed a metal handhold let into the stone, lowered his head, heaved himself up the steep step into the arch and cannoned out on to the narrow ledge beyond.

He staggered and grabbed the iron rail as the light hit him. He was on a level with the angels at the distant end of the nave. Steadying himself, hanging on tightly to the railing, he inched along, keeping his head up, breathing as evenly as he could.

There was a flash of blue in the archway ahead of him.

Matthew. He must have gone along the passage below and come up the other way into the south tower. John looked back. A man's arm was reaching through the archway, groping into space. He was trapped. He kept very still, gripping the rail. Perhaps the man was too big to get through.

Suddenly, he heard a gasp. Matthew had come out on to the ledge and looked down. He reached for the rail with both hands but, white and giddy, he began to reel and sway.

'Look up,' said John, firmly, moving towards him. 'Matthew. Look up.'

'I – I c-c-can't . . .'

'Yes, you can. Now. Look up. Look up, Matthew.'

Shaking and whimpering, Matthew did as he was told.

'Now step back. Go on.'

His head quivering uncontrollably as he tried to nod, Matthew stretched out with a foot and met thin air. He lurched sideways and hit the wall. He let go of the rail with one hand and found no grip on the stone.

'I can't . . . I can't . . .'

His knees were giving way, and if they did, he would slip under the railing . . .

'Shut up! Take a deep breath. Another. Now, step *back*, Matthew . . . behind you. One step and you're there. Step back.'

Closing his eyes, Matthew reached his foot backwards, much too big a step. His body was leaning forward out into space.

'Slide your hand back along the rail. Go on. Do it.'

Matthew pulled back, reached the doorway and collapsed. John heard him bumping against the wall as he slid down the stairs. He turned. In the north archway, almost bent double to squeeze through it, was the Earl's steward. He took a step on to the ledge, straightened up, smiling, and held out a hand.

'You're not safe here, boy,' he said. 'Best come down with me.'

His voice was so reasonable, so sane, John was almost tempted. Perhaps he had come up to help . . . perhaps this wasn't the man Matthew had been talking to. Then he looked into his eyes.

'I don't think so,' he said. 'I don't think I'm safe with you. Nor is Matthew. He knows you killed Hugh. And now I know too.'

The steward grinned. 'Got proof, have you?'

'No, but Matthew has. I heard what he said. And he's already going down the other way.'

'He'll say nothing.'

'I will.'

'I don't think so. I think I'd better come and get you, in case you have a little accident. It would be terrible if you fell, you and your young friend going to meet your maker both in such a short time . . . wouldn't it now? Such a tragedy . . .'

The steward edged nearer, reaching out so that the crowd below would think he was pleading with John to come to him. John backed away.

'Look down there,' said the steward. 'They're all looking up at you.'

'Are they?' said John, keeping his eyes on him. 'And at you too.'

'They'll think I've come to rescue you. A great hero. You know what the mob is like.'

The steward came closer, closer. John was right under the rose window now, the colours washing over him, crimson, ultramarine, gold. The steward shaded his eyes, suddenly dazzled as a beam of light flashed from the clerestory window.

'Don't be a fool, boy. You haven't a chance. Matthew's just out there, he won't let me down. Give me your hand.'

Cautiously, John looked round. Matthew was in the doorway.

John shook his head. 'Come and get me.'

Almost close enough, the steward pounced forward and Matthew screamed.

The steward started, whipping his head round. His feet went from under him and slowly, slowly, he rolled over the rail and plunged out into space, his satin sleeves billowing like huge wings. Below, the crowd scattered as he landed on the grey stones and lay still, spread-eagled like a shattered, gaudy bird, its neck broken, its feathers laced with blood.

John looked at Matthew.

'I don't trust you,' he said. 'Go down. I'll wait here till you call out from the bottom. Either that, or you'll have to come out here and get me.'

Still trembling, Matthew shook his head.

'And you'll tell the truth?'

Matthew tried to speak, but couldn't, just nodded, dumb and shaking.

'Go. Go on, go.'

Matthew turned and started to feel his way down the stairs. With a last look along the nave to the flying angels, John followed him and sat leaning against the archway, his eyes closed. He was tired, so tired. It seemed an age before Matthew's shout came from below. John wondered briefly why, after their first cry of horror, there had been so little noise from the crowd.

Halfway down, through a slit in the outer wall, he saw a strange light flickering on the grey wall ahead of him. He struggled up on tiptoe, but it was too high. With one last final effort he jumped. Reaching his arm through the slit and grabbing the far side of the wide sill, he pulled himself up and looked out.

Far below, the crowd was pouring across the square. Even further away, down the escarpment, the houses of the Jews were on fire.

Chapter 18

The rain came just in time, gusting in sheets down the hillside, beating against the walls and against the windows as they melted in the heat, swelling the little stream till it became a torrent spilling in through the doors, dampening the flames.

The crowd did nothing to help the Jews save their houses. They did nothing to help those trapped inside. It was the mob up from the city who had started the fires, though no one owned to it and no one challenged them.

John half-ran, half-fell down the stairs and out into the cathedral, where he ran into the arms of the Magister. In vain he begged to go to try and find Aaron to see if he was safe, but the Magister would have none of it. With as little fuss as he could manage, he got John away and into the vestry, where Matthew was already crouching in a corner, a sodden heap of snot and tears. The Magister pushed John down on to a bench.

'What now, John?' he said, his voice icy with rage. 'What further outrages are there to be? We should never have taken you in . . . it has meant nothing but disaster since you set foot in the door,' and he glared down at John's injured limb. 'Matthew was right. The devil is in you somewhere . . . I daresay it is *there* after all.'

John closed his eyes and slowly shook his head in disbelief. Outside, the rain was still drumming down and the sound of heavy wheels creaked across the cobbles. The Magister peered out of the door.

'Holy Mother of God,' he said, crossing himself. 'His Grace . . . the Bishop . . . come for the trial tomorrow.'

'Trial,' said John, jumping up, 'trial? What do you mean? They must set him free. Aaron's father didn't do it . . . None of them did. The Earl's steward killed Canon Senan. I don't know why, but he did. And he killed Hugh . . . he killed Hugh too and made the holes . . . the holes in his . . .'

He couldn't continue. The Magister wheeled round on him, hardly containing his fury.

'Sweet Jesu in Heaven, may you be forgiven. Lies now, lies to get you out of trouble, as well as . . .'

'Ask him,' said John, dully, subsiding back on to the bench with a nod at Matthew still cowering in the corner. 'Ask him. Ask why he was talking to the steward. Ask him why he said he was glad he'd done it. That's what he said – "I'm glad you've done it" – and the steward tried to shut him up. Ask him. He knows . . .'

The Magister stopped in his tracks. He looked at John then down at Matthew. 'What are you talking about?' he said, uncertainly, with a puzzled frown.

'Ask him,' said John again.

'Matthew? Is this true? What do you know of all

this? Why were you up by the rose window?'

But Matthew would say nothing. He scrabbled even further into the corner and turned his head to the wall. John put his head in his hands. Then he looked up. He took a breath and began again, trying to get the picture clear in his head.

'The steward came up to kill me. He told me so himself. He was going to make it look like an accident. He slipped and I didn't. That was the only accident.'

'But when did the steward say all this ... when did he speak to Matthew and say this – about killing you?' said the Magister. He did not hear the door to the cathedral quietly open.

'To Matthew? When he was standing by Saint Aelred's shrine and he thought no one heard. To me? Up by the rose window,' said John, 'just before he fell.'

'But why should he want to kill you – or anyone?' said the Magister, bewildered.

'I think I can tell you.'

Canon Gwyllim stood in the doorway. The Magister looked round at him, startled.

'Then is – is it true?'

The Canon nodded, his pink flesh pale now, seeming to hang in loose folds on his cheeks, dark rings circling his eyes.

'I will explain if I can,' he said.

He came into the room and sat on the bench beside John. John drew away from him, but the Canon simply put his hands together in his lap, looking straight ahead, seeing nothing.

'Not a hair of his head, John. Not a hair of his head did I touch. And now that he is dead, I will see justice done for him.'

John nodded. 'Good,' he said. 'At last.'

He looked at the Magister, who dropped his eyes, then back at Canon Gwyllim.

'Please . . . Why did he kill Hugh?'

'Money. We all owed the Jews money. But the rest of us just wanted them sent away. We didn't want anyone to die . . . The steward said he had a way to make the people rise up against them and drive them out . . . but I never dreamt . . . I didn't know he meant . . .' He bowed his head.

'And Canon Senan?' said John.

'The steward and his men . . . you will remember the Canon was at the door, praying. They hadn't expected that. They had to get him out of the way and get rid of him. Hugh followed the lamp into the wood.'

'I remember.'

'They had been going to take one of the boys on the way home, I don't think it mattered which, but Hugh came out alone. It was a gift.'

John gasped, horrified. 'It might have been me,' he said. 'I was going to go, but Hugh said he would be quicker. He died instead of me.'

The Canon looked at him without pity. 'No, not you. They wouldn't have taken you. A saint must be perfect. If you had gone they would have waited and taken someone in the wood.'

John bowed his head.

'I think they wanted Hugh all along . . . the Boy

Bishop . . . and undoubtedly . . . undoubtedly perfect . . . but one of the smaller ones would have done. A sacrifice. A ritual sacrifice.'

'Why didn't they kill him at once?' said the Magister. 'John says he was alive when he was in the wood.'

'So you believe me now,' thought John, 'when it's too late.'

'They didn't want marks on the body, only the hands. Still perfect you see. They only knocked him out and hid him. Then they returned and . . . and . . .'

'Please . . .' said John, 'his hands . . . did they really crucify him?'

The Canon shook his head. 'Thanks be to Christ, no. I think they smothered him. His hands . . . that was done later. Afterwards. He didn't know . . .'

There was a silence. John stared at the floor.

'And the Earl?' said the Magister.

The Canon shook his head again. 'I believe . . . I understand he knew nothing until it was all over. He may have guessed . . . I don't know . . . he may feel it was done partly in his name. He is sick with guilt now, they say . . .'

'Yes . . .' said the Magister. 'Poor Hugh. Poor Little Hugh . . .'

There was silence for a long time. John looked at the Magister. If they'd got there in time . . . But they hadn't . . .

Then the Magister said, 'One thing puzzles me still. Why . . . why was Canon Senan holding Hugh's hair when he died?'

Canon Gwyllim shrugged. 'I don't know. Perhaps

he had been holding it while he was praying.'

The Magister shook his head. 'I don't think so. His beads, yes, his scourge maybe, but not that . . . Someone must have put it there.'

John looked at Matthew, sitting against the wall now, his head on his knees, under the rack that held the gold crucifix.

'You did, didn't you?' he said.

Matthew didn't answer.

'It was you, wasn't it?' said John again, almost shouting.

Matthew nodded without looking up.

'You wanted it to look as if Hugh had killed the Canon and run away.'

Matthew went on staring into space. The Magister looked at him and shook his head.

'The Bishop is waiting,' said Canon Gwyllim.

'The Bishop?' said John.

'He wishes to see you. He has spoken to us all. He knows what happened.'

John looked at the Magister.

'I will come with you, John.'

'I'll be all right by myself,' he said, but the Magister stood up and opened the door. They left Matthew slumped by the wall.

The rain had cleared but the bushes dripped and water trickled in an endless stream down the path to the city. The Bishop had been kind but firm.

'Life will be difficult here for you now, John,' he had said. 'It was, after all, an accident that the steward fell, but some may try to blame you. You may stay in the school if you wish, as long as . . . as long as you keep silent.'

The Earl's steward was already laid out in state in the cathedral like the hero he undoubtedly would be. It was doubtful if Matthew would ever speak again but he was to be sent to the infirmary where he would be taken as mad if he found his tongue and tried to tell the story. The Earl's men who had confessed to helping the steward had been banished. No one was to say anything. No one.

A proclamation was to be made to announce the guilt of all the Jews. They were all to be expelled from the city and indeed had already left, thus robbing the crowd of the spectacle of a hanging. The King himself wanted to be rid of them for he owed them money too, like most of his wealthy citizens, and this was the perfect moment. What did the truth matter? The Jews were gone. And a new martyr would be no bad thing for the cathedral . . .

John hurried down the hill. The little house was still standing but blackened and scarred, the roof fallen in and the Star of David hanging crooked over the door. A rough, wooden cross was planted into the earth outside. John wrenched it out, broke it across his knee and threw the pieces over the wall. He went in and stood for a moment looking round. The room smelt of burnt timber; the walls were smeared with smoke and the table he had sat at with Aaron and his mother was nothing but a pile of ash. Someone had written 'Out with the Jews' with their finger in the dirt. He tried to rub it off but it smeared, and anyway who was to see it now? He turned away and slowly climbed back up the hill, not sure whether his foot or his heart was aching more.

At the top, he gazed and gazed across the flat, sodden, empty countryside. However small a group of them were left, he would surely have seen them moving from up here. Where had they gone? Was Aaron with them? Was he safe? He knew one or two had been burnt to death but no one knew who, and no one cared. They were gone and that was enough.

As he went past the cathedral he looked up at the little ploughman, plodding his way over the arch, his ugly face still grinning. John put up a hand and held him for a moment. A sudden warmth seemed to seep down his arm and he looked down into his palm, looking puzzled.

Suddenly, his face cleared and he hurried on, round the cathedral to the masons' yard. The sound of hammering seemed to rush out to greet him. Nervously, he pushed open the gate. Would the master mason remember him? He was inside, cutting a stone. He looked up.

'John. Good to see you. How are you?'

John gave a little grin and shrugged his shoulders.

'How's it going at the school, then?'

'So, so.'

The master smiled. 'I'll wager. Not what I would want. This is the way to learn, out here.'

John nodded. The master frowned.

'Wait a minute,' he said, 'I've been away a while. I was forgetting these . . .'

He put down his hammer and chisel, patted John

211

on the shoulder and went to a small, wooden shack in the corner of the yard. He looked inside, foraged around and came out with a leather bag. He held it out to John.

'Here,' he said, 'I've been keeping them for you.'

John almost snatched the bag, hugged it to his chest and swallowed. His father's tools. The tears he had kept at bay for so long threatened to spill down his cheeks.

The master gave him another pat. 'Thought you'd want to keep them,' he said. 'He was a good man, your father, a good mason.'

John nodded again, hard, not trusting himself to speak. Then, 'Th-thank you,' he managed. He shifted the bag to one hand and the tools clanged about inside.

'Careful,' said the mason. 'You'll maybe be needing them one day. You staying here now, in the school?'

'Dunno,' said John. 'No . . . I . . . I don't know.'

'I'd have you here, apprentice, but I've got my own two lads and there's not the call now the shrine is built.'

'Norway they've gone?'

'Who? Oh, the others, yes. There's a new cathedral building there – Trondheim. But that's a long way.'

'Yes. Well . . . thank you . . . thank you for the tools, I'm really glad . . .'

The master nodded and picked up his hammer. John came out of the yard. Quietly, holding the bag as carefully as he could so the tools wouldn't rattle about and be damaged, he went into the cathedral. As he did so, a group of canons came out of the vestry. Gravely they moved towards Hugh, gathered round him and hoisted the bier on to their shoulders. Chanting softly, swaying gently like a great ship on the ocean, they carried him down the aisle to where the west door was thrown open for Hugh's last journey through the city to his rest. The crowd was waiting outside for its latest martyr. John turned away.

'I thought I was the bit of a one for going off,' he said to himself and brushed his hand across his eyes. And now Aaron was gone too. He walked slowly down the aisle a little way and waited till the chanting faded.

'Oi!' came a whisper. 'Peg! 'E left this for you.'

John sniffed long and hard as Rufus came out of the shadows.

'I saw you come in. 'E said to give it yer.'

He held out his hand and John looked down. Screwed up in a ball in Rufus's fingers was a scrap of yellow cloth. Aaron's yellow badge.

'When?'

'S mornin' early. 'E come round with 'is guv'nor. They let 'im go. They didn't know where you was. I said I'd look out fer yer.'

John took it and smoothed it out, and a slow smile spread over his face. He'd got away. Aaron had got away and was safe. He had found his father and they had gone together.

'All right, then? Can't stop or 'e'll 'ave me arse.'

With a hefty clout on John's back, Rufus was away down the aisle.

'Oops, sorry . . . fergot yer back. See yer . . .'

John grinned. 'Do you know where they went?' he called.

'Nah. Didn't say . . .' and Rufus was gone.

John followed him down to the west door. He turned and looked back at the last angel.

'Shalom,' he said, with a smile. 'Well? Which way should I go, then?'

The angel said nothing, but the lift of its wings seemed to signify a kind of stone certainty that the great event that was promised would come and that it would be wonderful when it did. Its gold hair went on streaming out behind it as it flew across the vast space, and the lute looked as if it might come hurtling towards him at any minute.

'Which way,' he said again, this time to himself. One thing was certain, he couldn't stay here. Too many nevers, too many never agains . . . and not enough truth.

Where had they gone? Someone must have seen them as they left. He would ask and ask until he found them. And if he didn't . . . well, there was always Trondheim . . . He could get there, no trouble. Time enough to make up his mind when he got to the sea.

He gave the little ploughman a pat, hefted his bag on to his shoulder and, dot-and-carry, peg-leg, twister, set off down the hill.

A note from the author

The legends of William of Norwich and Little Saint Hugh of Lincoln both concern young boys found dead with the marks of the stigmata on their hands. These legends date from the late thirteenth century and seem to have been connected with the expulsion of the Jews from England in 1290. Certainly entirely unfounded accusations were made about the Jews. At that time, the Angel Choir at Lincoln Cathedral had not long been finished and many of the stonemasons who helped to make it then went on to work on the cathedral at Trondheim in Norway.

This story is based loosely on those legends but the Cathedral of Saint Aelred and the city in which John and Hugh lived are imaginary interpretations of more than one English cathedral and city. However, if you ever go to Lincoln Cathedral, you should go up into the roof and the west front to see how amazing these buildings are.

STEP INTO THE DARK

Bridget Crowley

The eerily-lit staircase seemed to hide not ghosts, but things and people that meant terrible harm. The balcony in the Hall seemed far away, like a beautiful dream he had to wake up from. Reality was home and getting up to the ninth floor unscathed.

Danger surrounds Beetle wherever he is. When he tries to protect Tamar, the beautiful young singer, he becomes a target for the bullies' violent games. And then there's the girl in white, who vanishes as mysteriously as she appears. Could she be a ghost – and if she is, why is she calling out to Beetle across the darkness . . . ?

'A highly likeable and accomplished first novel . . . briskly paced without being rushed, the story will engage readers with its real sense of urban teenage life.' Linda Newbery, *Times Educational Supplement*